A

HER PROMISE

By

Shenetta Marie

A Divine Production

Her Promise Copyright © 2011 Shenetta Marie

ISBN 10: 0578084732
ISBN 13: 978-0-578-08473-2
Editor: Doris Frawley and Rubina Sardon
A Divine Production logo by: nicolejaneen@gmail.com
Cover Design by: Dynasty's Visionary Designs

Library of Congress Control Number: 2012902733

First Printing June 2011
Printed in the United States of America

10 9 8 7 6 5 4 3 2 1

HER PROMISE

A Novel

By
Shenetta Marie

DEDICATION

I never thought losing you would have been so painful. I guess growing up I thought you would have always been there. In my heart I felt cheated as if it was too soon for you to leave me. We had unfinished business to tend to. Like our trip to Harlem to visit the Apollo Theater together. I'm still going to make that trip and I'm going to hold you close to my heart while I'm there. I promise you that. Even though my heart was in pain when you left I also know that you're not suffering anymore and know you're in a more wonderful place with our Father the Creator. I am very appreciative of the time He did allow me to spend with my Angel.

Jeanette Parker

ACKNOWLEDGEMENTS

First and foremost I would like to thank God my Lord and Savior. Thank you for creating Shenetta Marie.

My mommy Valarie Roundtree, without you I wouldn't exist. I love you so much.

My two Kings, Dwight Quinn III and Dionte Clemis, mommy loves you two rock heads more than y'all could ever comprehend.

Dwight Quinn Jr. aka Big Wight, I Love you BD.

My best Friend Rubina Sardon, who knows, accepts and loves me for who I am without any judgment or fault, love you Boo-Bna.

Tamira Adams and Jimmie Jermale Clemis my two siblings I can be myself with because that fake phony shit is for the birds, really. Love you Myra and Boo.

Jimmie Clemis Jr., I love you Brother.

Thanks to Doris Frawley for editing for me. Ivy Willis for encouraging me, telling me to stop reading and start writing, thanks Boo. Charvonne Grant for reading as I went along, begging for the next chapter.

Of course a big special shout out to Demario Hudson and Marlon Hudson. FREE THEM HUDSON BOYZ.

And to everyone who has ever entered and exited my life whether good or bad, because without any of you I wouldn't be who I am today, thanks.

Divine

Wonderful, perfect, beautiful, excellent, lovely, stunning, glorious, marvelous, splendid, gorgeous, delightful, exquisite, radiant, superlative, ravishing

PROMISE

A Declaration assuring that one will or will not do something; a vow

ONE

Divine sat in the VIP area of the Mirage on the Water down on the West Bank of the Flats supposedly celebrating her 21st birthday but she really wasn't in the festive mood. Everyone was there enjoying her party except for her and she really couldn't understand why. Just a week ago she was surprised with a new toy, a 2011 Black on Black 745 BMW. She had more clothes, shoes, purses and accessories than a department store itself, but still she was sitting at her own party looking like she had lost her best friend. Thinking to herself *this is some bullshit, why the fuck am I sitting here not enjoying myself at my own damn party.* Divine stood walked over to the bar ordered herself a double shot of Remy Martin VSOP, threw it back and headed for the dance floor. On her way she noticed everyone poppin' champagne or throwing back shots. She received some wuz ups, head nods, peace signs and Happy Birthdays, but she wasn't stopping to politic with anyone. She was about to enjoy the rest of her night out on the dance floor.

As soon as her feet touched the dance floor, the DJ gave shout outs to all the Gemini in the building and then started with his Reggae selections as if he had read her mind and knew that Reggae was her favorite music to dance to. Instantly she started winding and twisting her waist dipping down low and winding up slow with her eyes closed imagining she was at home dancing alone. This was her first time dancing in public because whenever she went out she kind of always stayed to herself observing her surroundings. Soon as she started dancing all eyes were on her. Her dance was so exotic and seductive that no one in the club could take their eyes off her. She even had the females' attention. She was what some called every man's dream and every woman's nightmare.

Divine stood at 5'7" 175lbs, small in the waist and very, very, thick in the hips. Not only did she have the body she was also beautiful in the face. Pecan brown skin, small almond shaped eyes, the perfect size nose not too big or not too small, thin lips, and a beautiful strong jaw structure with high cheek bones. She kept her hair rinsed jet black and cut in an edgy cropped cut to show off her facial features. She was what men in the 70's called a brick house. Tonight this brick house sported a black BCBG Max Azria mid-thigh silk-nylon dress, with Gucci leather booties, simple pair of one karat diamond stud earrings and a right arm full of thick and thin gold bangles all making her look like an Amazon Goddess.

Promise looked over his right shoulder to see what all the commotion was that had everybody's attention. Once he saw what everyone was looking at he hopped off his bar stool and headed straight to the dance floor.

Divine felt a strong hand on her wrist and knew exactly who it belonged to. When she opened her eyes and saw the evil upset look staring back at her she started to panic, "Don, what's wrong, what happened?"

Never responding to her line of questioning he led her off the dance floor straight to the VIP area gathered her things then walked her out of the club to his truck only saying, "Go home".

"Go home! What the hell you mean go home? Don, what the fuck is going on?"

"I'm not going to repeat myself." Was his only reply before slamming the truck door in her face mad as shit.

He walked back inside the club not knowing if he was coming or going. Once he got back to his bar stool he ordered himself three shots of Remy downing them one after the other. *What the hell was Baby Doll thinking? Shakin' her ass like that in front of all these motherfuckers* was all he was thinking to himself.

⨯⨯⨯⨯⨯⨯

At home pacing the living room floor, Divine dialed Promise's number repeatedly why she didn't know because all she kept receiving was his voice mail. "Okay let me call Sin then," she said out loud.

"Wuz up wit' you Twin? Why you dip from our party so early?" Sincere asked as he took another shot of Grey Goose to the head.

"I ain't dip shit. Promise crazy ass put me out. What the hell is up with your boy?"

"I can't even answer that for you Doll. All I know is I saw the nigga throwing back shots like they wasn't shit and you and I both know that the nigga can't hold liquor worth shit. I stepped to him asking him what wuz up but he said everything was cool. Then I asked about you and he said you was tired and went to the house.

"What! Alright Twin I'll get up with you tomorrow."

"Yup"

TWO

Everyone sat in their regular seats in attendance at the big house ready to get down to business. Well everyone expect for Divine. Her not being there had everybody with a questioning look on their faces.

After being about 15 minutes late someone finally spoke about her whereabouts.

"Man this isn't like Baby Doll to be late. Hell she is the one that's always here early talking about our asses being late. I'm about to give her a call," Sincere said as he picked up his phone dialing her number.

"What's up Sin? I was just about to give y'all a call."

"Why, you on your way or something?"

"Nawl, I'm going to sit this one out. We can hook up later and you can give me the updates then," she explained while looking over the breakfast menu in front of her.

With concern in his voice, "So why you not coming through, everything cool, right?"

"Yeah everything cool, stomach just messed up from last night. So I'm in the Muslim's Spot getting ready to eat me some food."

"You know we ordered food, so why the hell you just didn't eat here?"

"Cause I didn't want to sit around y'all all sick trying to discuss business and not being able to concentrate. I was just going to grab me something real quick and head back to the house, but I ran into one of my peps from Quincy so I'm going to eat here and kick it with him for a sec."

"Cool, just call me later when you're feeling better and I'll stop by your spot to fill you in."

"Alright, I talk to you later."

As soon as Sincere closed his phone Promise was on him. "Where she at, is she on her way?"

"Nope, said her stomach is fucked up from last night and she doesn't want to sit around us sick not being able to focus so she's sitting this one out. Said she's out having breakfast with a friend."

"What the hell you mean having breakfast with a friend?" Promise asked with his face screwed up.

"Shit nigga I don't know, I wasn't questioning her all like that. My main concern was to make sure she was cool. And come to think about it, why you didn't know she was fucked up and wasn't coming? Y'all do live in the same damn house."

Promise sat through the entire meeting with his mind somewhere else mad as hell. *Who was Baby Doll out with and not handling her fuckin' business?*

The meeting was adjourned with everyone leaving except for Promise. He really couldn't even tell what the hell went on in the meeting because his mind was on Divine. The main question rolling around in his head was who and what is so God-damn important that she was missing a meeting because he wasn't buying that sick shit. Then asking himself why is the (Who?) part of the question so important to him. Well he knew why. He didn't trust niggas around his Baby Doll even though he knew she could take care of herself. She was one of them. She treated niggas like they treated hoes but he still didn't like the idea of one of them finally making their way into her heart. Because even though she didn't know it now her heart belonged to him.

He thought back to the beginning. Remembering his first time ever seeing Divine. Her aunt and cousins had moved in next door to his family on 140th and Kinsman on his 10th birthday. And once he saw her he said Happy Birthday to himself. They introduced themselves to each other, her family and his. He stared at her saying she looked like a baby doll so that's what he began to call her and soon so did everyone else. The only problem was she was two years older than him and she had quickly adopted him as her play little brother, that and the fact that she only came over on the weekends because she actually lived on Quincy with her mother and grandmother.

Their families became close real quickly his mother and her aunt, his sisters and her female cousins, his brothers and her male cousins, and Divine with all the Green Boyz. She was different from all the other girls. She was a straight tomboy wanting to do anything and everything the Green Boyz was doing. Nobody could catch her with a damn doll or playing house with the girls.

She was with the boys jumping off garages on mattresses, throwing rocks at cars, building club houses, going bike riding in different hoods, and when they had become of age she was out trapping getting money with them. The Green Boyz always protected her and would kill something if any harm came her way. Especially Promise Dontae Green and Sincere Mitchell-Green. She was so tight with the Green family some would have thought she had their blood running through her veins and when her aunt moved away to another house she still made her way back to Kinsman County to kick it with the Green Family.

When she turned eighteen she and Promise had gotten a two bedroom condo in Beachwood together. He didn't see any reason for her to move in by herself paying all that rent and he was only sixteen so he needed her name on the lease anyway. He actually preferred her name on the lease. He might have only been sixteen but he had damn near been on his own since he was thirteen. He could have had any one of his clucks to put the condo in one of their names, but he wanted it in Divine's.

He smiled to himself thinking about the past but that smile easily faded now thinking about the present. Divine had missed a family meeting to be around a nothing ass nigga doing some nothing ass shit which was unacceptable in his eyes.

THREE

Divine sat at her kitchen island enjoying a vegetable omelet with cheese wondering how in the hell a week had gone past since the last time she had talked to or even seen Promise. She knew that she had been a little busy kickin' it with her nigga Black from Quincy for the past week but it wasn't that serious that the two wouldn't have bumped heads. They did live together which made her know that he was avoiding her and now it was time for her to find out why.

Once she was done with her breakfast she had to run straight to the toilet and throw up. *Damn I haven't had shit to drink in a week so why is my stomach still fucked up.* After throwing up she took a nice hot shower then she got dressed for the day. She really wasn't doing shit that day so she decided to throw on a pair of Bold Curve Levi Slim jeans, a wife beater tank top, and a pair of Une Plum wedges by Christian Louboutin. In her ears were her signature one carat diamond studs. She un-wrapped her hair and played with her crop style cut, grabbed her red envelope purse, and threw on some clear MAC lip gloss. Simple was always her motto. If a female went all out the way with all that make up shit and too many accessories she was trying too hard and in her eyes why make it hard when it's easy. With that she was on her way out the door to see what the hell was up with her Promise.

Leaving her condo she decided to take the long way back to the hood. Instead of driving straight down Chagrin she made a right on Richmond Rd to South Woodland. She loved riding down that street. South Woodland had the most beautiful homes with beautiful manicured lawns. Those were the home where legal money and stable families lived and that's where she wanted to be in a couple of years. Yeah she enjoyed the street life and the fast money but at the end of the night she always fantasized about having children and owning her own business doing the true American family life thing and not the street family life. Even though she wouldn't change her street Fam for nothing in the world. She hoped one day they could all sit back and be normal, whatever that was anyway because her life was never truly normal. She just hoped that one day it would be. Thinking about being normal made her snap back to reality, because that day sure wasn't going to be one, fucking around with Promise crazy ass.

She couldn't even think of any possible reason why he was avoiding her besides that bullshit he pulled at her birthday party. But she was over it and it wasn't even that serious that he couldn't show his face at the place he lays his head at night. It wasn't like him to hold a grudge, well at least not one with her anyway. She could admit though that for the past couple of months he had been acting a little weird. He had always been overprotective of her. All the Green Boyz were for that matter but lately Promise had been a little extreme with his shit.

꒰꒱꒰꒱꒰꒱

Riding down 146th street Promise was damn near run off the road at the stop sign on the corner of Milverton by this crazy ass broad driving a Dodge Stratus GT running her mouth on her cell phone. He decided he would play for a little while to kill some time and to get his mind off Divine.

He jumped out of his truck and walked up to the female's car, "Hey Sweetheart, you need to get off that phone running yo' mouth and apologize to me for running me off the road."

"Hold on girl let me check this dude real quick because I don't know who he thinks he's talking to." The yapping female said into her phone. When she went to so call check the guy the cat quickly caught her tongue. She couldn't believe her eyes *this nigga is fine as hell* she thought to herself.

"Excuse me, but are you talking to me?"

"Yes, I'm talking to you Sweetheart," He replied while standing in his cocky b-boy stance. He wore an all-black V-neck Gucci t-shirt, some hard cut Levi's, an all-black New York Yankees pro model cap and some black Gucci boots. No matter what time of year it was he always kept boots on his feet. He never knew when he had to stomp a nigga out. "So what's up Sweets, are you going to get out and say you sorry or are you going to keep running yo' mouth to that nobody on the phone?"

"Let me call you back", the female said into the phone. As she parked her car she thought to herself *damn this nigga sexy ass fuck and I don't even like yellow ass niggas.*

As soon as ole girl was out of the car she started apologizing "I'm so sorry, I really wasn't paying attention."

"It's cool Sweetheart as long as I can get a name to match that sexy face." *Sweetheart you ain't sexy at all just an average looking broad.* He couldn't keep his smile off his face. See he was a very observant man. He had seen ole girl speeding up and down Kinsman's 40's streets lately so he figured she was new to the area and he needed another trap spot.

"Well yes you can get a name. It's Carmen."

"Carmen huh, that's cool."

"Thanks and what's yours?"

"Donnie. So where yo' man at Sweetheart?"

"He's probably with his other girlfriend. And you where your woman at Boo?"

Looking at his watch he replied, "My Queen is taking care of business right now."

"Your Queen," she replied with a confused look on her face. She wasn't used to men referring to their women in that term.

"Yes, my Queen. Why is that a problem for you?"

"Nope, your Queen as you call her is your problem not mines. I told you I had a dude anyway."

"Well since that's settled we might as well exchange numbers and go on about our day because for real Sweets I need to get back to business."

Carmen left feeling like she was in love already. There was something about that nigga that made her want to call her dude and tell him to go and kill himself.

Promise walked away smiling thinking how the Queen term threw her off. It threw most females off. He didn't understand why women didn't know their rightful place in a man's life. It didn't matter either way. That was their hang up, as long as when the time came Divine knew her place in his.

As he walked away he saw his OG Pops and decided to stop and holla at him for a sec.

FOUR

On the other side of town Rob stood with his 9 mm in his hand staring down at his latest victim. The nigga been skimming money off the top of the packs he had been giving him and on top of that he heard he's been trying to holla at his bitch. He could have let the nigga live for the skimming he would have just beaten the punk up badly, but he went too far over stepping his bounds with trying to fuck with his broad. And if it's one thing Rob didn't play about, was his bitch.

"You know my nigga I ain't even about to draw this whole situation out because you and I both know what the fuck you did so go on and close your eyes while I send you to meet your maker and while you're there tell him I said what up." And with that he shot his victim dead between the eyes.

"Y'all niggas hurry up and clean this shit up," he ordered his goons. "We got shit to do."

He went into the bathroom to throw up his lunch. He wasn't throwing up because of the murder he had just committed. Hell murder was as normal to him as washing his ass every day. But lately he had been getting sick, and he had been tired as hell too.

He made sure everything was cleaned up properly so no evidence was being left behind then he sent his goons on their way. He really didn't feel up to being in the streets at that moment so he sent his brother Tone to handle them. He needed some down time so he decided he would pay his mother a visit.

His mother still lived on 80th and Golden off Cedar because she refused to move out of the neighborhood which she grew up in. Even with all the drugs and murders. He had bought her a house out in Cleveland Heights a nice suburban neighborhood but she refused to leave the house she had made into a home for the past eighteen years.

He walked inside his childhood home hating the fact that his mother refuses to leave. But what could he do about it? Tie her up and drag her to her other house? Hell no, she would see him coming and shoot his ass. She was just as much of a killer as her son that's where he got it from.

Sherry Hill had Rob at sixteen years of age and her second son Tone at eighteen. Their father was a snitch serving a thirty year sentence in a federal penitentiary. Her sons were only two and four years old at the time and she vowed back then that she wasn't raising no punks. She never took them to see their father because she didn't fuck with snitches and neither would her sons even if the snitch was their father. That's why she raised her sons to be loyal and heartless.

He crept up behind his mother giving her a big bear hug. Well he thought he was creeping because she felt his presence as soon as his feet touched her front porch.

"Boy what I tell you about sneaking around my damn house. I'm going to fuck around and put yo' ass six feet under if you keep playing with me."

"Ma please, you'll never hurt your first born."

"Whatever nigga," she replied turning around and returning his hug. "Now tell me what I did to deserve this visit this time of day?"

"Nothing I just wanted to see my favorite and only lady."

"Yeah, yeah, yeah," she responded while walking into her living room and getting comfortable in her lounge chair.

He followed behind her flopping down on the couch.

"Boy, have you lost your ever lovin' mind? Flopping yo' ass down on my couch like you ain't got no home training."

"I'm sorry ma. I've just been so tired lately and I've thrown up at least three times this week. I don't know what's going on with me."

"Yo' dumb ass probably got somebody damn pregnant. When I was carrying you yo' bitch ass daddy threw up more than I did."

"I don't have anyone pregnant. For one I don't fuck any of those hoes raw."

"Yeah I hear you talking but you better back track your foot steps and see if I got a possible grandbaby on the way."

"Yes ma'am, but I'm telling you that you don't."

Rob laid there watching television with his mother and he thought about what she had said. There was only one person in the world he cared about enough to even fuck raw and the only reason he did was because he was her only but still they always used a condom. He knew she couldn't possibly be pregnant because he hasn't fucked her in over three months and Dee wouldn't do him like that. She would tell him if she was carrying his child. *Nawl it couldn't be* was the last thing on his mind before he drifted off to sleep.

FIVE

Divine knew exactly where to find Promise. She parked her car behind his 2011 Chevy Suburban and watched him talk about nothing to some corny ass looking hoe. As she watched him she took in everything about his presence. He sure wasn't her little Don anymore. He had grown into a very sexy handsome young man. And damn he looked good in that all black. He was rarely found wearing any other color.

Standing at 5'11" 230lbs of nothing but muscle he kept his naturally curly hair cut low along with his full beard. His lips always looked so soft she just knew they felt as soft as cotton and he had the most beautiful light brown eyes that seemed to sometimes steal her soul whenever he looked at her in a serious way. She smiled to herself thinking *that's when she knew he meant what the fuck he had said and wasn't hearing anything else after.* His body was covered with so many tattoos she'd stopped trying to keep count. And at only nineteen years old he had seen and did more things than a thirty year old man. He also made sure that the world knew it. No one was to ever underestimate him and this went for even her. If she didn't know anything else she knew not to underestimate Promise Green.

He was a man of few words. He was never the one to have long drawn out conversations. He always said what he had to say, that's it that's all. He's also a man with little patience. And feelings, what the fuck were those? His mother always told him out of all of her sons he was the one born heartless. She used to joke and say he must not be her husband's son.

Promise noticed Divine the moment she pulled up but kept on with his bullshit conversation with the broad, still trying to avoid her. But he knew it was about time for him to pay the piper. He really thought she would have been hunted him down. He didn't think it would have taken her a whole damn week. But he was also grateful for the time because he had really been trying to get his head and his feelings together. He didn't understand why he flipped out on her at her party. He just knew he didn't like all the attention she was getting. Really everywhere she went she always captured all the attention but seeing her dance the way she was did something to him. He didn't understand why because he had seen her dance a thousand times but it was in the comfort of their home. And he knew she didn't even notice that he watched her.

Divine couldn't take the waiting anymore. She knew he was stalling and she was ready to find out why. She walked up to him while he was talking to OG Pops. She gave Pops his respect grabbed Promise's hand then walked him inside one of their trap spots. As soon as she walked through the door she politely asked the four soldiers who were there bagging and tagging the product to leave, but no one budged. And that's when she lost all patience. She had already sat outside waiting for Promise to finish up his bullshit conversations and now these fools wanted to test her.

"I didn't muthafuckin' stutter, I don't give a fuck about what y'all doing. Now get the fuck out." She yelled with much bass in her voice.

With that being said everyone stood to leave giving her their apologies on their way out of the door. The only reason they didn't jump the first time was because Promise had just finished chewing their asses out about being behind schedule about a half hour ago. But none of that mattered because they would rather get chewed out by him than feel the wrath of Divine.

Behind her Promise stood smiling to himself. He loved to see her not taking any shit ordering niggas around.

Once the door was closed, she went at it, "Why the hell haven't I seen or heard from your ass in a damn week?"

"Why the fuck are you missing family meetings? Not handling yo muthafuckin' business."

"What the fuck does that have to do with anything? I told Sin I wasn't feeling good. I had gotten the updates and I handled things on my end. And that ain't why you been tripping because if it was you would have brought your ass home when you left my damn party that you put me out of. Now let's get to that."

"Nawl, let's get to you having some bullshit breakfast with no fuckin' bodies."

She breathed deeply, "I was going to have breakfast by myself but I saw my nigga from Quincy. Damn Don. We sat and ate together catching up on old shit. It wasn't about nothing."

He walked over to the couch to sit saying "Yeah that's what yo' mouth say but don't let me find out some other shit Doll. And so that you know I'm doing my homework on that nigga. So if you feel the need to tell me something you need to let that shit be known now," as he gave her that look that always stole her soul.

She knew he was tip toeing around what the real problem was. If he was doing his homework on a nigga he already had his answers which were nothing because she wasn't doing shit wrong. If she was playing with the ole boy, what the fuck did he care for? That wouldn't have been the first time she had a friend. And if he would have heard some shit that wasn't to his liking she would have read about her friend in the newspaper fucking around with Promise psychotic ass.

"Don it was breakfast, that's it that's all. And all I want to know is why you made me leave my own fuckin' party?" She yelled while staring him dead in the eyes.

He knew why he made her leave and now it was time she knew also so she wouldn't pull the bullshit no more.

"That's old shit just know next time your ass is out don't be out on no damn dance floor shakin' yo' ass like you some kind of hoe." With that being said he stood and went into the bathroom because he had to piss so fucking bad.

She couldn't believe what the hell she had just heard. She went right in the bathroom with him while he stood over the toilet taking his piss. "Negro, I know you just didn't call me a damn hoe?"

"No, I said shaking your ass like one."

"Don, I wasn't doing shit but dancing and you ain't ever had a problem with me dancing," she dictated to him while crossing her hands across her chest.

Flushing the toilet and washing his hands he told her, "You're right and that's because you're usually at home, not in a place full of people staring at yo' ass."

"You think I give a fuck about people staring. It was my fuckin' birthday and everybody was having a good time except for me. I wanted to enjoy myself, and I like to fucking dance so that's what the fuck I did." Now screaming at him as she walked behind him and watched him sit his arrogant ass back down on the couch like what she said didn't mean shit.

"I don't like people watching you!" He yelled banging his fist on the coffee table.

She stared him directly into his eyes and finally saw what she had been avoiding for all of her life why she didn't know. Maybe she did but didn't think it was possible. He was her Don, her little God in his own right. But now here he was all grown up and he damn sure wasn't little anymore. He hadn't been for the last couple of years now. She knew all along deep down in her heart why he made her leave. She guessed she just wanted to hear what he really felt come out of his mouth for a change. He had never been the one to bite his tongue but for some reason when it came to her she knew he kept his lips tight and right now wasn't going to be any different. So she thought she'd finally say what she had been feeling and let the cards fall where they may.

She sat down next to him on the couch. She laid her head on his shoulder grabbed his hand then intertwined her fingers with his wondering where she should start.

"Don, I'm not stupid. You could care less if someone looks at me. Hell, I think you love it. You love the fact that niggas chase behind me and me not paying their asses any attention. And if I do shoot my shot with one it isn't about shit but something to do. What your real concern is me letting some nigga into my heart and into my world." Once she said that she felt his hand tighten around hers so she put her other hand on top of his for some reassurance.

"Don, I haven't met any man out in these streets yet that could hold my attention and that might have a lot to do with you. I compare any and everybody to you. Don't any of them get money like you, them niggas in their mid-twenties and still haven't accomplished what your nineteen year old ass has. Those niggas want to fuck with me just because they want to be in my presence. They think they're in love with me but it's just the thought of it. They don't know my pain and my darkest secrets. They don't know why I can't sleep after a certain time at night and if they did they wouldn't even be able to handle that shit. Do you think they'll stay up to the wee hours talking, watching movies, or just bullshitting around with me until I felt comfortable enough to fall asleep? Yeah they want to fuck with me but do you think they will put me first in any and every aspect of their lives? No they won't but you will. Let's look back on it, when I came to you about my darkest secret you was ready to put the nigga down but you didn't out of respect for my wishes. Do you think them niggas would kill for me? I think not. You bought me my first car when I was sixteen and you didn't even have one. Do you think any nigga in this world would buy a female a car and he doesn't have one and not to mention a female that he's not even fucking?"

She cupped his chin tilting his head towards her. "Don, I see you baby. I see the things you do for me and I know why you do them. At first I just looked at them like it was nothing because we have always been so close and did everything for each other. But then you started doing and saying things that only a woman's man would. And just in case you haven't noticed I haven't had a nigga in my presence within the past three months now and that's out of respect for you. Lately I've noticed how you have been changing towards me and I believe I'm changing towards you also. So just like you've been watching me, I've been watching you. And on that note I'm going to get ready to leave because we're both dead wrong, it's time for business not pleasure. I'll see you at the house and if you try not bringing your ass home tonight, when I come looking for you tomorrow it won't be pretty."

With that being said she stood to leave, but he stopped her by pulling her down on his lap wrapping his arms around her. He put his hand behind her head and led them to their first kiss. And what a kiss it was. All she could think about while his lips were on hers was how she knew his lips felt as soft as cotton.

He broke his lips away rubbing his hands in his hair while getting his next statement clear in his head because he had to make sure she had it clear in hers once he said it. "Divine Nanette I love you. I always have and you know this. I will give my life to save yours. But I also love yo' ass enough to fuck you up if you try to go against the grain. You know how you like that attention bullshit sometimes so don't play with me. Do you understand me?"

"Yes I understand you and I love you too. And while we're at it what's up with ole girl I just seen you talking to?"

"Nothing much, we need a new trap spot. The one on 144th is getting hot."

"Speaking of that my boy Black was telling me about how much money there is down on Cedar."

"Why didn't you already know about how much money was down there? You were fucking one of them. I ain't forgot about you and that nigga. So nawl you're not fucking around down there."

"I was fucking him and getting his money. Not worrying about his business and where he got it from because I didn't want him in mine. And for your information he doesn't even hang on Cedar no more. He do his shit over in Hough Heights."

"Are you sure because you know that nigga got some type of sweet spot for you and I don't have the time or the patience for y'all bullshit."

"Yes Don, I'm sure."

"Well then I'll see if I feel it will be profitable. Then we'll handle that."

"Okay then I'll see you later. I'm about to go kick it with Ma Innocence for a while, alright."

"Before you do that, you said it's been about three months?"

"Yeah about three months maybe a little over and let's not forget that it wasn't an everyday thing anyway. Just about every blue moon." She responded while standing, rubbing his head and beginning to walk away.

He stopped her from walking away and proceeded to unbuckle her pants. She tried stopping him, "Don, come on now can't you wait 'til later when you get home remember business before pleasure."

He got her pants loose then slid them down to her ankles and took them off along with her shoes. "This is my damn business and you go let me taste you now, we can fuck later." And with that he slid off the couch and got down on his knees to serve his Queen. Once he got face to face with her pussy he couldn't believe his eyes. "Damn Baby Doll, yo' pussy fat as fuck." He spread her lips and his heart melted. This was what he had been waiting for his entire life. He had loved Divine from the first moment he had laid his eyes on her and now that she is giving him his shot he just prayed and hoped he didn't fuck it up.

She could feel him stalling once again and knew why. While guiding his head to the place she had been wanted him to be she leaned her head back. "Baby, trust me you won't fuck up. You've waited too long and if you do slip and fall a couple of times. I promise I'll hear you out and be understanding. Because even though you're a God to me I do know that you're only human."

With that there was nothing else to be said. Promise finally blessed his Queen. He dove in head first tantalizing her pussy. He sucked and licked her clit until she started shaking and cumming in his mouth. Getting down on her knees looking into his sexy eyes and seeing all her juices on his lips and face she couldn't help but want to get a taste for herself. She started molesting and raping his mouth loving the taste of her own juices.

"You know that's my pussy you got between your legs. Now don't fuck wit' me Baby Doll." After speaking those words he led her into the bathroom by the hand so he could clean his pussy.

Once she was cleaned and dressed she knew it was time to let him get back to business.

"Okay Baby I'm about to get ready to go, I'll see you later on."

As she walked out of the door he yelled behind her, "Tell mommy to make me a cheesecake while you're there and send them niggas back in here so they can get back to work. We're already behind schedule. We got to get this money. Daddy has to get his Queen out of that condo and into one of those big ass houses on South Woodland that she is fantasizing about all of the time."

"How did you know about that?"

"Come on now Baby Doll. I know your every move and every thought so make sure you remember that."

"Yes Daddy I'll remember and I will make sure I relay your message." With that Divine left to go on with her day.

SIX

It's been an entire month since Divine told Promise she wanted Cedar for herself. Now he felt it was time to get down to business. He and Sincere had been sitting on the corner of 79th and Cedar inside the parking lot of Cedar Finest Beverage store on and off for the past week. They were watching how the Cedar boys ran their operation. From where they sat they could see who the captains were, who the lieutenants were, who the street soldiers were, and how many corners they ran.

He was so surprised that they hadn't been a target for someone else by now. The niggas were too comfortable. Their whole operation was being run carelessly. Their main supplier didn't switch routes. Same shit day in and day out. Their foot soldiers kept the same stash spots. He was starting to think that this was going to be the easiest take over ever and a very profitable one also. *These stupid careless niggas got a goldmine on over here.*

"Man Sin, these niggas getting money over here. This entire hood is full of fiends." He said as he rubbed his beard.

"Yeah they are and we don't have to venture too far out our comfort zone. And these niggas slangin' our type of product, we go' have to make this shit happen soon."

"That's for sure. But what's up with you and that little female you met? Is she cool?"

"She's cool. She works at that Key Bank on the corner of 140th and Kinsman. I don't know how I haven't bumped heads with her before."

"That's cool that she's got a job we could use a square in our circle. What's her name?"

"Cherokee, she's from that 131st side of Garfield. Man, P, she got the prettiest chocolate little girl I have ever seen in my life. If I would have fucked her before nigga I would swear on a stack of bibles that was my baby girl. I ain't lying to you, she got my skin color and when she smiles big that's mine too. That shit is crazy. How can a kid I ain't never known or seen before look like me? Even Cherokee said it. I took them out to lunch the other day at The Bone Yard out there on Mayfield. P, I'm telling you we had a good ass time. I ain't played arcade games in forever. The Fam gone have to kick it there on some just having fun shit. Games, food and liquor, yeah that's what's up. I'm kind of feeling ole girl but you and I both know I got to take her through the ropes for a second. But fuck all that my nigga, I see you finally locked Doll's ass down."

Promise rubbed his hands down his face, "Yeah something like that, but I'm kind of feeling suspect about some shit though."

"What do you mean you feel suspect, like about what? Nigga didn't y'all just get together? And it ain't like she was out whoring around or something."

"I don't know man. I just got this crazy ass feeling. I really think she's pregnant man."

"Nigga what the fuck are you talking about? You mean by somebody else?" Sincere asked turning to get a look at Promise in his face.

"Yeah man, her ass has been getting sick since her birthday. But her body hasn't been regular in the past couple of months anyway. And you know I wasn't getting the pussy yet."

"How in the hell do you know how her body's been? Like you said, you just started gettin' the pussy."

"You ask me no questions and I'll tell you no lies my nigga. That's my business." Promise said as he turned the ignition to his bucket. "Let's go we've seen enough."

"No we didn't!" Sincere said as he tapped Promise's arm. "Look across the street. Isn't that Detective Barns and Detective Johnson sitting over there in that Magnum?"

Promise squinted his eyes to get a better look at the two men. "Hell yeah that's them. What the fuck them muthafuckas doing down here? This ain't their jurisdiction."

"I know right."

"Dem scandalous money hungry niggas probably on some bullshit."

"Promise, you know we're going to have to tail them sorry ass bastards. We got to see what they're up to."

"Nawl we ain't go tail 'em, not yet anyway. We'll put Diamond on their asses. She can get a couple of those chicken heads that follows her around on them. Keep them occupied for a while."

"That's what's up!" Sincere said holding out his fist for a pound.

Staking out Cedar watching their whole operation was so tiring but it was also needed because they got a lot of info out of it. But now all Promise wanted to do was to go home and crawl in between Divine's legs and stay there for the rest of the night.

He couldn't get enough of her. He had been fucking hoes in the streets since he was thirteen years old, but none of them meant anything to him and they damn sure didn't have a pussy like his Baby Doll. He still couldn't get over how fat her pussy was. He had never seen anything like it. And the taste of it alone God-damn it drove him crazy. He could eat her pussy for breakfast, lunch, and dinner and the way she controlled her pussy muscles was heaven sent. That's why it wasn't her pussy anymore, it was his personal heaven.

He hated the fact that he procrastinated so long in getting with her. He hated knowing that there was someone else out there that knew about his heaven. And what he hated the most was that's the person who taught her to learn her body and do all those tricks with her pussy that he loves so much. But he tells himself it's cool because he will be damned if that nigga or any other nigga will ever have another taste of Divine.

On his way to the house he decided to give his mother a call because he hadn't talked to her all day. And that wasn't like Innocence not to call and check up on her baby.

He was his mother's oldest and favorite son. She named him Promise because when he was born she promised to love him despite the horrible way he was conceived. Promise knew part of the truth and he carried her pain, sorrow and regret on his shoulders.

He loved his mother more than life itself. Even after she married the man that betrayed her gave him his last name and had four more kids with him. Promise didn't care though. He knew her husband/baby daddy couldn't stand the sight of him but all that didn't mean shit to him all that mattered to him was that his mother loved him without any fault and unconditionally. But growing up he made sure he gave her husband hell. It was his fault that his mother was put in the situation that got her pregnant in the first place. If he decided to accept her with her child growing inside of her, Promise felt he shouldn't have treated him any different than the rest. So he returned the favor and gave the man hell. None of his siblings knew the truth. Promise wasn't even sure if Innocence knew that he knew part of his history.

After leaving his mother a message telling her to give him a call, he made his way home. He figured his mother was asleep because she always went to bed every night around ten.

SEVEN

Standing in front of the mirror Divine admired her body while smoothing on her lotion. She heard the bedroom door ease open and started taking her time with the lotion making sure she didn't miss a spot because she knew Promise was watching her.

Promise couldn't take the show anymore so he walked through the door and hugged her from behind. "Baby can you wait a minute and let me put on something sexy for you?"

Backing her to the wall, "There's no need for all that."

She loved his aggressiveness. She had no say so when it came to him wanting her. He always took what he wanted and when he wanted it. There were no ifs, ands, and buts about it.

With her old partner it was always on her terms, she never let him control her. She never wanted him to think he had her like that. If he ate her pussy it was because she wanted it. If she let him fuck her it was because that's what she wanted, never because he wanted to. He could have never called her and said he wanted to fuck and if he had that would have been the end of their so called friendship. And the crazy part about it was he never even tried to be aggressive with her. She guessed he knew his place and if he wanted to keep her coming back he knew he'd better stay there.

And now that she and Promise had finally got their emotions together she loved every minute of it. He wouldn't even give her body a chance to go in need. In the past four weeks he had trained her body to do his bidding. She knew he still had hang-ups about not being her first. Sometimes when she moved her body in a certain way she would see that crazy shift in his eyes. But what he didn't know was that she had a crazy imagination and she wasn't just always fantasizing about houses. She'd also been fantasizing about him and what she would do to his dick when they finally crossed the line.

The moment he touched her as he backed her up, her pussy started gushing. He eased his hand down between them and started rubbing her clit. She felt so good that she started biting him on his chest because the way he was making her pussy feel was ridiculous.

Her legs started shaking which made him stop. "Don what the hell is wrong with you. I was about to cum," she exclaimed while trying to put his hand back between her legs.

He pushed her hand away grabbed her by the waist and led her to the bed. "Not yet, this my heaven and she will cum when I'm ready for her to."

And that's the shit she loved. She swore she could cum just from the way he talked to her.

As they reached the bed he pushed her down telling her, "Spread 'em."

She did as she was told spreading her legs slowly and as wide as they would go. On his knees admiring what belonged to him he spoke softly. "This is the fattest pussy I have ever seen in my life and damn I love the way it smells. This is my pussy and don't you ever forget it. Do you hear me Mommy?"

"Yes Daddy," she responded anticipating what she knew was coming next.

As always he dove in head first making sure every word he had said she now felt. He licked her clit up and down real slow and then he circled his tongue around it even slower. She couldn't take the torture as he teased her so she grabbed his head pushing his face in even further begging. "Baby please make me cum. I've been waiting to feel this all day."

He stopped licking, removed her hands from his head, grabbed her thighs even tighter, pulled her towards him, and looked up into her eyes. "Didn't I tell you this is my heaven and I say when she cum not when you want her to. Do you understand?" And with that he was back burying his head into her pussy now closing his lips around her clit sucking and taking greedy pulls. And as soon as he started moving his tongue from side to side real fast on her clit she started screaming and squirting all over his face. She couldn't believe how he made her feel. Looking down at her King she thought *damn I love this man*. She pulled his head up toward her face, and looked into his sexy eyes asking, "Do I have permission?"

"I don't know, I don't think you deserve to taste any of this."

"Please Don, you know I do. I've been waiting on you all night."

"You sure it's been me."

"Dontae, please stop questioning what I feel. It's been you my entire life."

Staring down at her he knew in his heart she was speaking the truth, so yes he would grant her permission, "Take what you want."

With that being said she grabbed his face and devoured his mouth. She loved the way her pussy tasted on his lips and as she sucked on his lips and tongue, he pinched and twirled her right nipple knowing it was connected straight to her clit, making her pussy cum all over again.

He guided his dick inside her pussy after she came down off her climax. She threw her head back, savoring her favorite part of their sex, him entering her. Stroking her long and slow he whispered in her ear, "You're my queen, my earth and my life." Speeding up fucking her harder and deeper he gasped, "Damn, Doll I love you and I promise that I will never hurt or leave you. This pussy feels so good and it's all mine."

She didn't know whether she was coming or going. She threw her head back and held on for the ride. Her heart felt as if it was going to jump out of her chest and she was moaning so loud she would have thought someone else was there in the bed with them, because there is no way that could have been all her. She gripped his dick tighter making her pussy muscles pulsate. She knew he loved when she did that. She started throwing her hips back at him making him pant even louder. Yeah he controlled their sex life but once he entered her it was her show and that dick belonged to her. He put her right leg over his shoulder leaving her left leg down flat between his legs. She grabbed a hold of his neck and threw her pussy at him as if her life depended on it. Once she started pulsating her pussy muscles again he couldn't take it anymore. He started cumming shooting his hot nut deep inside of her. When she felt his seed her walls gripped even tighter and she started screaming and cumming along with him.

Getting himself together he looked down at his Queen. Staring her dead in her eyes he felt he needed to let her know some things. "I swear if another nigga ever feel what I just felt I promise you will regret it. Do you understand me?"

Out of breathe she answered, "Yes Don."

He grabbed her chin making her look into his eyes. "Yes Don my ass. Do you understand me Divine Nanette Dawson?" He asked staring at her with his eyes stealing her soul once again.

She knew he was dead serious because he never called her by her full name. He hated her last name. She rubbed her hands up and down his back loving every inch of him and making sure he knew he had her attention she whispered, "Yes Don, I understand you."

Kissing her on her forehead and climbing off of her he got out of the bed and held out his hand. "Come on let's go clean my heaven."

While in the bathroom getting cleaned she started to feel sick again. As soon as Promise finished drying her off she had to rush to the toilet and throw up.

"Don, I don't know what's going on with my stomach. I have been getting sick since my birthday, and I haven't had anything to drink since that night."

He gave her a questioning look. "What did you eat today?"

"Nothing really because lately I haven't had much of an appetite, it's like food makes it worse."

"I don't see how that is because your hips are spreading for sure. Or maybe I'm just fucking you that good."

"I know you didn't just call me fat," She said while throwing a towel at him.

He grabbed and hugged her tight. "No I didn't say you were fat. I said your hips are spreading but it's looking good on you."

"What the hell ever Don, you just hurt my feelings."

"Well I apologize for hurting you Baby. Now go brush your teeth so we can get some sleep. Maybe your body is just tired."

After she finished up in the bathroom she climbed into bed beside Promise. As soon as she got in the bed he pulled her to him wrapping his arms around her neck putting her face in his chest and throwing his leg over her body. That was their way of sleeping every night. She couldn't even go to the bathroom without him holding her tighter and asking where she was going.

EIGHT

Waking up to the ringing of his cell phone Promise rolled over in the bed bringing Divine with him as he reached for his phone on the night stand. He turned laying on his back and tucking her in his right arm. He picked up his phone realizing he had ten missed calls. His uncle Freaky, his brother DeAndre, his cousin Sincere, and damn even his youngest brother Dontez all called. *Damn* he thought, it must be some shit going on. And if it was some shit that urgently important he also needed to wake Divine.

"Baby Doll wake up," he said while shaking her.

"What's up Baby?" she asked stretching.

"I don't know Ma. I got ten missed calls from the Fam."

Now that sounded odd to her because the Fam never called like that and back to back. This means they were having a big problem if they're trying to reach him like that. So she reached over to her side of the bed grabbing her phone from the night stand. When she opened it she saw she had just as many missed calls as he did. "Baby, hurry up and call somebody back because I have missed calls in my shit too. Something is really wrong if they couldn't handle it themselves.

He decided to call his Uncle Freaky first to see what was up.

"What's up Unc? Talk to me quick. The way y'all blowin' up a nigga's phone got me a little shook."

"Innocence is having a money problem. She went to the freak show on St. Luke Dr. and her beeper went off, but those nasty ass strippers do have tips for us though. Nephew did you hear me?"

"Yeah I heard you. I'm on my way to put some money in her pocket now." Promise responded while hanging up the phone.

"Baby Doll, get up and throw some clothes on. We got to roll."

"Talk to me Don you're starting to look like your daddy. And when you start showing your devil side I know it's something crazy. So what's up?" She asked while sliding out of bed.

"Innocence is at St. Luke hospital. Unc is there with her but he said she don't look too good. She was beaten real badly and her heart has stopped once already. But he said he may have a couple of tips for us. So we up!"

"What the fuck did you just say?"

"You heard me. So like I said, we up!"

As they rode the elevator to the eighth floor of the hospital there was nothing but silence and serious faces. There was no talking between the two because regardless of what anybody had to say war was about to begin in the city.

As soon as Divine saw Ma Innocence lying in the hospital bed fucked up she knew she had to be the one to take charge. She knew all Promise saw was his life lying there and knew he was ready to go rogue. He was more of a doer. Shoot now and ask questions later. She might have felt like that at times but she was a thinker also. She looked at every aspect of a situation and in this one she saw one valuable thing.

She walked up to Uncle Freaky and told him to clear the room. She didn't want anyone else in the room, not even Innocence's damn kids.

After asking everyone to leave there had to still be one loud mouth in the bunch.

"What the fuck you mean leave the room? That's my damn mother lying in there," Tez screamed with hatred in his eyes. "Because Promise and Divine finally decides to show up, now it's time for every fuckin' body to leave."

Freaky pulled Tez to the side and looked him in the eyes, "Now is not the time nephew. Ain't shit going to get solved with you in here about to start acting like a spoiled ass baby."

"Oh I'm the spoiled one. It's cool, I'm 'bout to blow this joint anyway. Niggas go bleed for this shit right here."

Promise stood over his mother looking down at her with tears in his eyes. Who on this God's green earth would be stupid enough to touch his mother? He has been in the streets for years, killing niggas just for fun and going to war on GP. Out of all that no one was dumb enough to touch his life. This just didn't seem right to him. There was about to be a lot of slow singing and flower bringing because the city of Cleveland was about to bleed.

Divine stood on the other side of the bed looking at Innocence in another world. No one in this world would fuck with Promise's mother so she figured this damn sure wasn't about any beef, war, or business.

As Uncle Freaky walked back into the room, Divine spoke with authority in her voice. "Unc, this shit is personal not business. Therefore I don't want anyone in this room, not even her seeds."

"Start talking Baby Doll", Promise said looking up from his mother.

"I'm not saying we're invincible because I know everybody bleeds. But you can't tell me a muthafucka is dumb enough to pull this shit. Look at her Promise," she said while pointing at Innocence. "That's an act of hatred. Whoever did this to her tried to beat her to death. An enemy would have just shot her and got it over with."

"Damn Doll, you're right." Freaky whispered while rubbing his hands down his face.

"Yeah I know, therefore I don't want anyone near her. I don't trust any fuckin' body. So sorry to say Unc you're on door duty 'til we figure this shit out."

She bent down to give Innocence a kiss on the forehead and whispered in her ear. "I know you're too strong and too stubborn to die on us, so hold on. Whoever did this is going to die, trust me."

"Freaky, what are the doctors saying?" Divine asked while walking over to the side of the bed Promise was on.

"They just said she's fucked up real bad, but she will live. They have her heavily sedated so she won't be in any pain. They don't know if she can hear us talking to her or not but said it would be a nice thing to do."

"How long are they going to keep her drugged up? When do they think she'll be able to wake up and talk?" Promise questioned as he wrapped his arm around Divine's neck.

"They don't know nephew. They just said we'll take it day by day."

"Alright then Unc we up, got to hit these streets."

"Y'all keep me informed."

Promise kissed his life then grabbed his heart hand and walked out the door.

"Oh yeah Unc, you heard Baby Doll. Nobody! I don't care if it's her fuckin' mama. And no police tell them we don't know shit!"

"I got you nephew."

NINE

As soon as they left the room Divine went into the bathroom to make some calls.

"Hey, Vine, I was just thinking about you."

"What's up Ma? I need to know is everything cool over there with you and grandma?"

"Why? What's going on?"

"Ma, would you just answer me please."

"Everything is fine. We're sitting here watching American Idol and the house is locked up tight."

"Cool, I'm going to send someone to check on y'all. I'll be by there tomorrow, okay!"

"Okay Baby. I love you!"

"I love you too Mommy!"

"On to the next one," Divine said while dialing another number.

"Hey beautiful, it's that time already?"

"No, but I need a big favor."

"Anything"

"Some bullshit done happen to my peoples and I need you and only you to go look after my mother and grandmother. Just make sure they're cool and do a couple of rounds. If you see anything suspicious kill on sight."

"I got you, but soon as you get a chance come holla at me. If something is so serious is going on I need to know more. I can't have anything happening to you."

"Yeah I hear you, just do what I asked for now." She hung up the phone not having anything else to say.

Walking out of the bathroom Promise was there right in her face. "Is everything cool? Are you sick again?"

"No, I'm good."

"I know you Baby Doll, so tell me, is Mommy okay?"

She just smiled because he did know her so very well. "Yeah she's cool. She said her and grandma watching TV and everything's locked up tight. I told her I'll be by there tomorrow."

"Okay then let's get this show on the road."

They both rode in silence for about twenty minutes before Promise decided to speak.

"Talk to me Baby Doll. What you think this shit is about?"

"First of all I know this shit ain't business because who would have the balls to touch your mother? Second of all, why weren't any of our spots hit?

"You're right Doll, but where do you think we should begin? Who'd have a personal problem with, Innocence?"

"That I don't know. But honestly I think we should start with home."

They rode to Innocence's house because they knew everybody would be there possibly looking for some leads. When they got in the house the first person they saw was Promise's sister Destiny. She was sitting on the couch crying her eyes out.

"Where is everybody at?" Promise asked as he took a seat next to his youngest sister putting his arms around her.

"Dre and Diamond is up in mommy's room. Haven't nobody seen Tez since he left the hospital. You know he's in the streets trying to find answers. And Sincere is on 140th at the big house having a family meeting with y'all peoples."

"Promise, you know this is all y'all fault!" Destiny shouted pulling out of her brother's embrace. "If y'all weren't in those damn streets slangin' that bullshit nothing would have happened to my mother. All y'all care about is money and having a name that everyone fears. Now look what it has cost us, our mother laid up in the hospital fighting for her life."

He looked at his baby sister. He truly wasn't in the mood for the back and forth shit. Whenever things were good everybody had their hand out for their cut. But as soon as something goes wrong it's his entire fault for being in the streets. He wasn't about to sit around and listen to her bullshit. He had just broken her off three thousand dollars for a New York trip so she could go school shopping with her friends. He definitely wasn't going to listen to this bull.

"Yeah whatever, you just make sure you keep mommy's house clean till she gets back." With that being said he went to holla at his other siblings.

When he walked into his mother's room he couldn't believe his eyes. Whoever fucked up his mother also fucked up her room. He was thinking how right Baby Doll was. This was personal because nothing else in the house was fucked up.

Divine sat on the edge of the bed with her head resting in her hands. Dre sat on the dresser in deep thought and Diamond sat in her mother's favorite arm chair.

Diamond spoke with a soft voice to her big brother because she was mentally tired. "Brother whoever did this was looking for something and whatever it is it has to do with mommy. Not your shit."

"Yeah, that's the same thing Doll said. She said this shit was personal because nothing or no one else was touched."

"I'm with y'all on that one," Dre said while jumping off of the dresser. "So how are we going about this?"

Divine looked up from the floor asking, "Dre, where the hell is Tez?"

"Man I don't know. He left the hospital all mad because y'all put everybody out. But I know why y'all did it and I understand. Tez is a fuckin' hot head and that nigga been acting real strange lately. I don't know what's up with our brother."

"Well it's about time we found out. We have been giving his ass too much freedom." Promise chimed in.

"I agree with you Promise." Diamond said while standing up from the chair. "I got the room. I'll get everything cleaned up tonight. Y'all can go home. We'll hook back up tomorrow."

"You sure you don't want me to stay and help you clean?" Divine asked

"Nawl, you cool. Go home and take care of my brother, because I know he's about ready to kick in every door in the city. There ain't any point of y'all going to war when it seems this is some inside shit. I got everything on this end."

Divine smiled and gave Diamond a hug, "Yeah you're right. You know he has no understanding of anything. But you know why that is. He's a man, they don't think like us females."

"What the fuck? Y'all are standing here talking about me like I'm not in the fuckin' room," Promise said while smiling at them.

Smiling back at him Divine walked up to Promise giving him a hug and kissed him on the cheek. "Baby we was just fuckin' with you. Let's go home and we'll start fresh tomorrow."

"Yeah you're right, let's ride."

"Why no one has answered my fucking question," Dre asked aggravated as hell.

Promise looked at his brother and he admired him. Dre was growing to be more of a gangster and more heartless than he was. "Well bro since we're figuring it's an inside job we're going to handle everything in house, but we're still going to knock on a couple of doors. It wouldn't be right if we didn't."

"That's what I wanted to hear Big Homie," Dre said while giving his brother a hug.

They said their goodbyes and left Diamond to tend to their mother's room.

There wasn't any question about where Dre was going. He was going to find Tez and put his foot in his ass.

TEN

Divine lay awake in Promise's arms not able to fall asleep. She was thinking about her visit with her mother tomorrow. She didn't want to scare her mother with the Innocence thing but she needed her mother to be on point. She would surely die if anything bad happened to her mother because above all her mother was her world.

Her mother had her when she was fifteen years old. Her mother told her that her labor was so horrible that she swore she would never have another baby. So needless to say she grew up as an only child. She was spoiled rotten by her mother. They went everywhere and did everything together. Her mother was more than a mother to her. She was also her best friend/sister. She guessed it was because her mother had her when she was so young.

But having a child young didn't stop Victory Walden. She finished high school and landed herself a permanent full-time position at NASA Glenn Research Center by the time she was nineteen. Thanks to the school summer program she participated in at East Technical High School. Victory made sure her daughter had a good life. All she ever wanted was to see Divine happy. That's why what her daughter wanted, she got.

Divine smiled to herself thinking of the time spent with her mother. Those times were the highlights of her life. Her mother gave her that ounce of love that she still had in her heart because her father fucked up the rest of it in the worst way.

Her father Jason Dawson aka JD was seventeen years old when Divine was born. But unlike her mother he didn't stop there. Now that she was twenty one her father had twenty children. But Divine was his first child so she stuck to her father like glue. She was his so called favorite. So anything she wanted just like with her mother, she got.

Her father started off in the streets as a stick up kid, then he was a pimp, and by the time Divine was eleven years old her father was deep into the drug game. He supplied ninety percent of the cocaine flooding through Cleveland streets. By Divine being his first and favorite he taught his daughter everything about the streets and the game at a young age. No one was going to get anything over on his first born. He taught her how to drive a car at the age of twelve years old telling her, "just in case". He taught her how to cook, weigh, and bag dope by the time she was fourteen telling her, "just in case". Whenever she would fall asleep in the car he would wake her up saying, "Fat Momma you must always stay awake when someone is driving so you can know where you are. You must always be aware of your surroundings." Therefore when the Green Boyz started trapping she had already known the rules and regulations of the game.

Her mother never knew what her father had instilled in her. Their time was their time until one fucked up night at 2:33am. Her father attempted the ultimate betrayal. The one man, who was supposed to love and protect her from all harm, the one who taught her about the streets, the one who taught her that men weren't shit and not to trust anyone, was the very same one who tried to steal her innocence away from her. She wasn't having it though. She was half raised by him and she'd been running with the Green Boyz for about two years. So needless to say he wasn't going to get the very thing he had always taught her to cherish and protect. And that's what she did, protected herself. It was just a shame that it had to be against her father. From that one fucked up incident he made her the cold hearted, trusting no one, don't give a fuck about you bitch, which she was 'til this day.

She told no one of that night except for her Promise. And once he was told he was ready to body her father. But she didn't want him dead not yet anyway. She knew he would get his and she wanted to make sure he was alive to see it.

※※※※※※

Promise knew Divine wasn't sleeping, he could tell by the way she was breathing. He hugged her a little tighter and rubbed his hands through her hair. He then lifted her chin so he could get a good look into her eyes.

"What's on your mind Baby Doll?"

"Nothing"

"Don't lie to me. Are you forgetting I know you better than you know yourself?"

Looking into his eyes she could feel him deep in her soul so she knew he deserved the truth. "Well honestly I was having a blast from the past and right now I really don't want to talk about it. But I would like say that I love you. Don, you're the reason I can sleep at night. I don't wake up at the same time every night anymore thinking I'm going to be violated. You give me peace. Baby, you keep me sane and you've helped me to repair my heart. So I'm asking you please don't be the one to destroy it again."

He could see the hurt and fear in her eyes and he hated it. He hated knowing how those feelings got there in the first place. She was so beautiful. Everything about her personality, her spirit, and her soul. And she very well deserved better than the hand that she was dealt. In her eyes he could see the spoiled child who was use to having everything her way. He could see the frightened little girl scared to let anyone close to her. He could see the daughter who loved her mother with her very soul he could also see the hungry ambitious money maker she had become. But deep into her eyes he could see the cold hearted bitch that she could sometimes be. He could see the she-devil in her heart and he could also see the killer part of her all because one man had fucked her over.

"Baby, I know your story and I know why you're so distant at times. I understand your ways and know where they originated from. I know why you have that wall built around your heart. And you also know I'm not that nigga that's going to sit back and wait for your wall to finally fall and for your heart to accept me as your man, not just as your Lil Don. Divine Nanette, by me knowing these things about you I would never by any means break your heart and I would never do anything to hurt you. Now that I have your heart in my hands, you can trust and believe I'm going to keep it safe. Divine you should know by now that I love you more than life itself. I would never do you dirty because it will kill me to see you hurt and me being the cause of it."

She felt overwhelmed. She knew what he just told her was straight from his heart. She couldn't even speak. She didn't want to speak. All she wanted to do now was serve her King.

She pressed her body all the way against his rolling him over and sliding on top of him. She straddled him looking down at him. Looking into his eyes all she saw was the love he had for her not the devil's son who he really was. She leaned down and gave him soft kisses on his lips. While kissing him she could feel him getting excited and aggressive, but tonight it was her turn. She held his head still and nibbled on his bottom lip. She started nibbling her way down his body stopping to pay close attention to his nipples. When she ran her tongue across them he got excited again grabbing her arms trying to turn her over.

She stopped him, "No Don, let me play for once."

She started her way down his body once again, hoping she could make it to her destination. And once there Divine was in awe. She saw his dick all the time but never this up close and personal. He never let her venture too far in their sex life. He always had to have complete control. But now that she has made it this far she loved what she saw. He had to have the most beautiful dick in the world. And she have seen her fair share but none of them made her want to do what she was about to do right now. Her mouth watered just at the sight of his dick.

"I can't believe you would deprive me of this," she moaned while grabbing his dick taking her first sensual lick of the head. She licked around the head again and again and then she opened up her mouth and slid his dick inside.

She was sucking his dick for the first time but she knew this was something she was going to be doing every day. At first she just sucked and played with the head but she wanted more. She opened wide and slid her mouth all the way down on his dick until it touched the back of her throat. "Mmmmmm", she hummed while she vibrated her mouth on his dick.

He rubbed his hands in her head guiding her to please him just the way he liked it. But as soon as he felt his dick at the back of her throat for the second time he couldn't take it. He needed to be inside her.

Before she knew it her mouth was pulled off his dick. She was pulled up to him so that her pussy was right over his dick. Then she felt it in a way she had never felt it before. He was ramming his dick in her while she was on top of him. He gripped her hips and guided her up and down his pole forcibly.

She tried to grab his hands so she could take control of the ride but he just wouldn't let her. He dug his fingers into her hips even more making her bounce up and down on his dick even harder. Before she knew it he was coming deep inside her.

He pulled her down to him hugging her tight telling her how much he loved her.

She didn't know what to feel. That was their first time ever having sex that was painful to her and the first time they had sex and she didn't cum. She didn't know what had gotten into him but she didn't like it. Yes he was always aggressive and controlled their sex but he always made sure he pleased her. Tonight was something different.

He held her tighter feeling like he was floating on cloud nine. He couldn't believe how good her mouth felt on his dick. What she was doing to him was sinful. He couldn't take it. He had to bury himself deep inside her. He loved the way her pussy felt around his dick. And once he felt her pussy muscles tighten up on him and she screamed his name it was all over for him. He came good and hard. But what he didn't realize was that the scream he heard was from pain, not pleasure.

Promise fell asleep feeling like the King that he was. But Divine still lay awake in his arms trying to understand how her night started out with her thinking of her past and him having a wonderful talk with her to let her know that she can relax, he got her. He made her feel like she wanted to love on him all night long. But now all she wanted to do was crawl away from the love of her life and sleep in the fetal position.

ELEVEN

Cruising down Quincy in her 2006 Black on Black Chevy Impala SS Divine sang along with Ashanti, thinking of Promise.

And when the world start to stress me out,
Where I run
It's to you boy without a doubt
You're the one, who keeps me sane, and I can't complain
You're like a drug you relieve my pain, May seem strange
You're like the blood flowin' through my veins,
Keeps me alive and feed my brain
Now this is how another human life,
Could have the power to take over mine
Cause you're mine
Baby, baby, baby, baby, baby

Even though she couldn't understand his actions last night he was still her baby. Always had been and always will be.

She made a left on 82nd and Quincy going towards her childhood home. Driving down her grandmother's street she couldn't believe how much the scenery had changed since she was a little girl. A lot of the houses were torn down or boarded up because of the crack epidemic. And damn even the neighborhood corner store was gone.

"Now when did that happen?" She asked out loud to herself.

She waved to some little kids as she drove down the street and as soon as she pulled up in front of her grandmother's house she saw his white 2011 745 BMW sitting there looking sexier than a muthafucka. *He must have sat outside the house all night making sure nothing budged.* That was one quality she liked about him. Even though they were just friends he always made sure he looked out for her.

She walked up to the passenger side window and gave a light tap.

He had seen her when she first pulled up. He stalked her while she made her way up to his car. When she tapped on his window he looked up at her and admired what he saw. She was the prettiest female he had ever seen, and even though he couldn't have her as his woman he did cherish what they had. He smiled at her while unlocking his doors so she could enter.

"What's up big head?" She asked while leaning over and giving him a hug.

"Shit! Now talk to me about what's going on."

"Some fucked up shit happened to my God mother so I just wanted to make sure everything was cool with my mom's. I didn't expect for you to sit here all night. I just wanted you to check up on things. So there wasn't anything strange going on here was there?"

"Yo' ass knew I was going to stay when you called. But um there wasn't anything going on just the same ole routine. Man, grandma is making a killing over here."

"Yeah, that she is. But I need to go in here and holla at them. So thank you and I call you later when I'm finished with them."

"Alright, I'm about to go to the house and catch a couple zzzzzz. But as soon as you're done come by the house I have some other things to discuss with you."

"Okay!" She responded while getting out of the car

As she started walking in her grandmother's yard she heard, "Hey big head, you look like you're putting on a couple of pounds. But it looks good though."

She couldn't believe what the hell he just said to her. So she gave him the finger and went inside to see her mother and her favorite.

"Hey ladies, what are y'all doing?" She asked walking through her grandmother's door.

"Nothing, grandma is in the shower. She made you your favorite breakfast. It's on the stove." Victory told her daughter while looking through her purse.

She walked into the kitchen and instantly lit up. Her grandmother made her some salmon patties, grits, cheese eggs, and biscuits. She fixed her plate and walked back into the dining room to sit down with her mother.

At the very moment she sat down she heard a tap on her grandmother's window.

Standing up she said out loud "Damn already, it's only 9:00 o'clock in the damn morning."

She walked into her grandmother's room and went to the window. She saw one of childhood friends, Tommy looking back at her. "Boy, what you doing over here this early in the morning?"

"What's up Vine? I should be asking what you doing down here this early."

"Well nothing, just kickin' it with my family. So what can I get for you?"

"Let me get a pint of that Hennessey."

"Alright, hold on." She got the bottle and put it in a brown paper bag and went back to the window.

"Do you want some cups?"

"Girl please, you know I ain't using a damn cup." Tommy said as he passed her the thirteen dollars.

She passed him the bag through the window and took the money "Alright T, it was good seeing you."

"You too Vine, don't be so much of a stranger you need to come kick wit yo' peoples some time." He responded while walking down the driveway.

She went back into the dining room ready to enjoy her breakfast. Once she sat down her mother was on her with the questions.

"So girl you better get to talking. Got me over here scared and worrying about you. What the hell happened that you got that boy over here sitting outside our house all night?"

"I'm going to be honest with you ma but I don't want you freaking out going crazy, okay?"

"Okay."

"Well somebody broke into Innocence's house and beat her half to death. She's in the hospital now heavily sedated for the pain so she can't even tell us what really happened."

"Oh my god, Is she going to be okay?"

"Yeah, the doctors said she is going to be fine. I didn't want to take any chances with you and grandma. But we think it was someone she knew, someone with something personal against her. Therefore you won't see anyone sitting outside the house all night. But I will be coming over more, sitting with y'all more often."

"I understand and I am so sorry about Innocence. What hospital is she at so I can go see her?"

She told her mother which hospital Innocence was in and she also informed her to make sure she gives her a call before she goes so she can let uncle Freaky know.

"Oh yeah Vine, did you know they found Robin's son dead in an abandon house over on Cedar?"

She gave her mother a questioning look, "Robin who?"

"My friend Robin, you know her son Black. Now stop acting crazy."

"What? It's not that Mommy, I was just with him about a month ago eating breakfast. Man, this shit is crazy. Do they know anything?"

"Nope baby, his mother and his brothers are taking it real hard too. Out of four boys he was the baby."

"Dang mommy, Black was my boy. Tell his mom to let you know if she needs anything, I got her. And did they have the funeral yet?"

"She didn't want one. She said his body wasn't recognizable so she just cremated him."

"Damn," Divine said while shaking her head. She couldn't believe her boy was gone. And why, Black was cool with everybody. "Well don't forget to tell her what I said."

"Okay baby and you make sure you are careful. I don't know what you are doing, but I do see all the shit you got. So just be careful please."

"Yes mother," she replied getting up and giving her mother a kiss on the cheek.

Once her and her mother finished talking her grandmother finally surfaced from the bathroom.

"Hey grandma thanks for the breakfast."

"You're welcome baby. What you about to get ready to do?"

"Nothing really, why what's up?"

"I want you to take me to George's store on 74th. I need to fill my liquor order."

"Okay and someone came by and got a bottle of Hen. I put the money on your dresser."

"Alright, thanks baby I'm about to go get dressed."

TWELVE

Promise floated Divine's old school Chevy Impala up Kinsman and smiled thinking about her and her love for Impalas. Whenever Chevy changed the model she just had to have one. And he made sure he made it happen. She owned a 1963, 1995, 2000 and a 2006, all in the SS model and custom made in her signature black on black. He really didn't even know why he got her the 745. Shit she has only driven the thing once. And that was on her birthday.

As he drove he figured he needed to go to the house and check on her. They'd been missing each other at home for the past week. He had been so busy in the streets taking care of business and going to the hospital to see his mother. Every time he walked into his mother's room his Uncle would tell him that he just missed Divine. And when he got home at night she was already sleeping which was odd for her. He kind of got a feeling that she has been avoiding him and it seemed she has gotten away with it because he has been so damn busy. Shit, he hadn't even felt his Queen's insides at all this week. But that ends today. He's never too busy for Divine or his heaven.

Before he went home he wanted to stop and have a drink with his nigga Jaz. His boy had been telling him to get at him for the past week. He pulled in Whitmores parking lot hopped out of the car and went inside to see what was up with his boy.

Jaz sat at the bar talking to some hoe he was trying to get some ass from. Once he saw Promise walk in he waved him over and dismissed the female.

"What's good P? I've been trying to get at you for minute."

"Shit, just been a little busy. You know taking care of shit." Promise responded as he sat on the bar stool and nodded his head to the waitress so she could bring his norm.

"Well, what I wanted to holla at you about was your brother Tez."

Jaz saying that got his attention real quick, because no one had been able to catch up with his brother. "What's up? You saw him somewhere or something?"

"I mean I really can't say what's up with him. I was just a little concerned. I saw him down the way on 30th by my baby mama's spot. And he just didn't look right."

With his head to the side and a serious don't fuck with me look on his face, "What you mean don't look right?"

"I mean like sick my nigga. And you know what I'm talking about. I really ain't trying to get in yo' family business but I know that's your lil brother. So a nigga just throwing caution to the wind, you know. I mean I would want somebody to pull my coat tail on some shit like that. You know when people are close to you we kind of miss the signs. You feel me?"

"Yeah I know and thanks. A nigga really needed that info. Now you say on 30th right?"

"On 30th"

"Once again thanks my nigga," Promise said as he threw his shot of Remy back and proceeded to walk out of the door.

Now a million things ran through his mind, but first things first, Divine.

When he walked through their door he threw his keys down on the table and began to call her name. "Baby Doll where you at?" He asked as he walked down the hall of their condo.

When she didn't answer it kind of had him worried but soon as he reached their bedroom he heard the shower water running. Walking into the bathroom he stood outside the glass shower doors lovin' the sight in front of him.

She felt him watching her but instead of her putting on a show like she always did she hurried up with her shower and stepped out.

He grabbed her towel so he could dry her off but instead she took the towel out of his hands. "Thanks baby but I got it this time."

He looked at her like she had lost her damn mind. What the fuck did she mean she got it this time? He took the towel away from her not saying a word but letting her know with his facial expression that he had it.

She wasn't in the mood for even a slight disagreement so she let him have his moment. Honestly she did miss him doing those little things for her. So she stood there enjoying the feel of him drying her off. When it came time for him to dry between her legs she stopped him. "Don, I'll get that part. I'm kind of, you know."

Looking at her like she just lost her mind once again, "you're kind of what?"

"I'm bleeding, well not really bleeding just spotting. So I will dry your heaven today."

He couldn't believe she had said that shit with a smile on her face like it was nothing. He looked at her. She returned the stare trying to figure out what was going on in his head. The way he was looking at her had her a little on edge.

After about a three minute pause he finally spoke, "Baby Doll, if you don't stop playing with me and open your damn legs."

Usually she would stand her grounds with him. She would give him a run for his money but not right now. She really hasn't been in the mood for being her bitchy self and she could see in his eyes that he was not to be tested. So she just opened her legs so he could see for himself.

He took the towel and dried his heaven. After he got a couple of good wipes he decided to take a look at the towel. When he saw a faint pink spot on the towel another million things ran through his mind. His evil twin was trying to surface but this was his Baby Doll right here he's dealing with. So he really had to focus because he didn't want to have to tear up their whole damn condo starting with her ass.

He grabbed her hand and walked her out of the bathroom. When they entered the bedroom he walked over to her dresser and grabbed a pair of her panties. He went back into the bathroom opened a drawer and got out a panty liner. When he got back to her he had already put the liner in her panties. He kneeled down in front of her with the panties so she could step into them.

The whole entire time she watched him it kind of scared her but at the same time she felt grateful for him. She didn't even realize he knew where she kept her feminine products or to even know what to do with them. But then she thought about it, this was Promise. He always paid close attention to her. And like he always said he knows every move she makes.

Once he pulled her underwear up he pulled her close to him and wrapped his arms around her getting his mind together. He tilted her head back and gave her soft kisses on her lips.

As he kissed her lips she melted of course. She had been so busy trying to be mad at him for the other night that she didn't realize how much she missed him. When he slid his tongue in her mouth her little lady started gushing as always. Now she was really mad that she was spotting.

He pulled away from their embrace and led her to the bed. Once she was seated on the bed he got down on his knees in front of her and laid his head in her lap. He was really trying hard to get his thoughts all the way together and not flip the fuck out on his Baby Doll.

While his head was in her lap she rubbed her hands slowly on his head then made her way to the top of his shoulders. He was so tensed and she understood why. His mother was in the hospital, he was still taking care of the streets, and he hasn't had a slice of his heaven in a week. Now as she rubbed on her man she felt childish for dodging him.

She thought about their situation. She knew when it came to her in the bedroom he had to be in control. He had to have her when and how he wanted her. He let her control so much of everything they did in their lives even before they made it official. When it came to the streets if he was making a decision she didn't like she took control. And he always let her. When anything was going wrong he went to her for advice. And he always let her have the final say, no matter what.

Some could say he was soft for it but hey doing things her way kept their family out of jail so far. So why did she have a problem with him controlling the bedroom. Yeah that night was a little rough but that was Promise. Sometimes his sex was rough and at other times it had been so soft and sensual it would bring tears to her eyes.

She decided the silent treatment had gone on long enough. "Don, you know I love you with all my heart and I apologize for all the distance between us lately."

With his head still in her lap, "That's not even where my head is right now Baby Doll. Tell me, how long have you been spotting? You know it's not your time of the month yet."

Still rubbing his shoulders, "Well, it's been going on for about a week now. And yes I know."

"So you don't think anything is wrong with that, you don't think you need to call the doctor? And you say about a week. We had sex on Friday night and it's now Friday again. So could you please give me an exact day?"

"Don, do you want me to be honest?"

"That's the only way I want it, good or bad."

"Well Baby, sex was a little rough the last time we did it. The next morning when I woke up my stomach was cramping and that's when the spotting started."

"So you're telling me I'm the reason?"

"That's not what I'm saying. I'm just telling you when it happened."

Now standing up in front of her looking down at her he asked her one simple question "Do you want to know what I think?"

"Yes Don please tell me what you think. Even if I don't want to know you're going to tell me anyway."

He put his hands in his pockets. "Don't start that smart shit. Trust me with the shit I got on my mind you'll want to tread very lightly. Now for the past couple of months you haven't even had a real period. All your body was doing was spotting anyway. And there's no need for you to ask me how I know. Since the day after your birthday I know you have been sick throwing up here and there. You haven't had an appetite but yet your hips are spreading."

"Don, what are you getting at?"

"Just listen to me Divine. You have been laying around sleeping nights away something that you don't do. Now you're trying to tell me that a little pounding to your pussy something you be begging for got you bleeding. And through all of this you still don't have any clue about what can be wrong with you?" He asked staring into her eyes.

"For real Baby no. I just figured my periods weren't heavy because of the stress I've been going through. Me sleeping now at night I associated that with you. And far as you keep calling me fat I honestly don't see it my clothes size hasn't changed."

"Yeah whatever Baby Doll, now I'm going to tell you what the fuck I know. Your ass is pregnant and I know for a fact it's not by me because this shit started before we even fucked." He yelled at her while staring into her face.

Staring back at him she couldn't believe what he was accusing her of. "Don, there's no way I could be pregnant and not by you at that. Before you I always used condoms. And before you I haven't fucked in about three months. So that would make me about damn near four, four and a half months now. Don, there's no way."

Pointing at the phone he yelled, "Get yo ass on that phone and call your doctor. I want to be sitting in front of her tomorrow. I don't mean two three days from now, but tomorrow."

"Okay, damn Don you don't have to yell."

He walked into the bathroom and took a quick shower. When he came back into the bedroom she was still sitting in the same spot with her head down in her hands. He got in on the other side of the bed and turned the television on. He tried to ignore her sitting there but he just couldn't. How could he she was his heart, his world. If she was pregnant it didn't happen on his watch. It was before their time as a couple. But it was still fucked up. His heart was about to bring another man's child into this world because he was not allowing her to get an abortion.

All he could say was *"Damn"* about the situation. "How long are you going to sit there? I'm trying to relax." He asked her as he stared at the back of her head.

She turned and matched his stare with sadness in her eyes. While he was in the shower she thought about everything he had said. And he might be right. She had heard of women having menstruations while they were pregnant before. She still didn't know how because she had always used a condom but she also knew they weren't a hundred percent. Now the only thing that was going through her mind at that moment was *what was going to happen between her and Promise?*

"What, you want me to leave out of the room?"

"No, I want you to get on that phone like I said. Then I want you to get in this bed and relax your man. After that I want you to go fix me something good to eat. Yo' ass ain't cooked shit in weeks."

She did exactly what her Don had told her to do. She called the doctor and had an appointment scheduled for the next day at two o'clock. After she hung up her phone she crawled into bed and gave him some of the best head she could to relax him enjoying every minute of being able to play. She loved having him in her mouth and him being the one crawling up the walls for a change. When she was done she went to the kitchen to make him some shrimp scampi, a baked potato, a garden salad, and a wheat dinner roll, with a tall glass of Tropical Punch Kool-Aid.

Anything for her King!

THIRTEEN

"Today is a good day" blasted through Rob's car speakers. He bobbed his head up and down to the music rapping every single verse. He felt like today was going to be a very good day for him. The sun was shining, birds were chirping, kids were playing, and the streets seemed to be quiet. He hasn't had any drama with his money and he had a big shipment of heroin coming in later on that day. *Yeah today is definitely going to be a good day*, he thought to himself.

He rode down Central on his way to Fairfax Recreational Center. Today they were having a basketball game, Central vs. Cedar. When he turned right on 82nd and Central the street looked like Crenshaw Ave from the movie Boyz in the Hood. Everyone was out chilling on their cars and the park benches. Little kids were playing on the slides and the swings. Him seeing most of the DTW together having a good time really put a smile on his face.

He hopped out of his car and proceeded towards the basketball court. As he walked he had all the ladies' attention. Standing at 6'2" 220lbs of nothing but cockiness, sporting a bald head, with a set of the juiciest lips covering a perfect set of white teeth, Rob had to be the sexiest brown skin nigga in Cleveland. His smile alone was enough to brighten anyone's day. It seemed as though whenever he walked into a room panties fell at his feet. He knew most of the hoes in the city wanted to fuck him and yeah he had run through enough of them. But only one female had ever kept his attention.

Once he reached the court he saw his brother Tone. He gave him a hug and some dap. "What's up? Who's winning the game?"

"Man, you know Cedar's running the muthafuckin' show." Tone responded while opening his bottle of Pepsi.

Rob grabbed his brother's pop out of his hand and took a swallow "That's good, you know I got a couple of dollars on this."

"Hey, big Bro guess who I ran into the other day?"

"Who?"

"Jay. He was walking down Golden on his way to Candy's house."

"How's he doing, he cool right?"

"Yeah he cool, but he told me he was hungry and needed to eat."

"Did you put him on?"

"Yeah I did, but at first I didn't want to. I didn't want Dee coming around here going postal on us about her lil brother."

"Man, she'll be cool. I can't see her getting mad about him getting money. Shit their father is a get money nigga."

"Well everything's good, I gave him the 82nd corner to work." Tone said as he snatched his pop back from his brother.

"Nawl, give him 79th in front of the beverage store."

"Yeah, okay."

Cedar whooped Central's ass in the game. But it was cool because everyone had a good time kicking it together.

✖✖✖✖✖✖✖

Sincere sat in his car across the street from Fairfax enjoying the game. But that wasn't the reason he was down there.

Down the way consisted of a lot of hoods. They had 89th, 86th, Quincy, Central, Cedar, and Hough. Then it went to the projects Garden Valley, King Kennedy, Outhwaite, Case Court, Carver Park, Unwin, Longwood, and 30th. And each hood was filled with a gang of niggas.

By DTW having a hood event he could see how many of them actually united together. If they were going to take over Cedar they needed to know how many niggas had Cedar's back. And by sitting here observing he could also tell who was real niggas, bitch niggas, wanna be niggas, gangster niggas, and even fuck boy niggas.

He could tell by the caliber of these niggas he's looking at right now that they might just take over 89th to Hough, not just Cedar. But he needed to holla at one of niggas from Longwood because he didn't want to step on their toes.

Picking up his phone he called his nigga Fox.

"What's good Sin? A nigga ain't heard from yo' ass in a minute."

"A nigga been busy, but what's good wit' you?"

"Shit, on my way inside Curtis's store to grab some shells."

"Well I want to ask you something."

"Shoot my nigga."

"What's up with y'all other half of down the way?"

"You're talking about them Cedar niggas and shit?" Fox asked while walking into the store.

"Yeah all of them, 89th to Hough"

"Ain't shit up, them niggas up there and we down here. Shit nigga we barely get along with each other down here, you feel me? Why what's up?"

"We heard niggas getting money over there so we talking about a takeover. And I didn't want to cross none of my niggas you know?"

"Man those niggas ain't getting money up there. The only hoods that is seeing something is Cedar and Hough. Now the niggas over there gettin' that bread, I mean mad dollars."

"So they're not associated with none of y'all Longwood niggas?"

"Nawl my nigga they're fair game, do what you do. Shit, let a nigga know what's really good. So a nigga can get in on that wit y'all. But if I was you I would check with yo' girl Divine also. You know Quincy is her original stomping grounds. So a couple of them niggas might be her people."

"Alright, but what you getting into tonight? You trying to go to Tops and Bottoms, put them singles on those hoes?" Sincere asked as he pulled his car away from the curb.

"That's what's up. Hit me up around 10 o'clock."

"Yup" Sincere said while hanging up and thinking to himself how Divine was the one who ordered the takeover.

✂✂✂✂✂✂✂

Rob saw the cherry red Dodge Challenger pull off and thought to himself that the guy driving looked familiar, but not from around his way.

"Hey Tone did you see that Challenger that just pulled off?"

"Yeah, why"

"Do you know who it belongs to?"

"Nope my nigga, but I did see it in the parking lot over on 79th by the Urban Store before."

"You saw it. What was the nigga doing?" Rob asked now a little aggravated

"Shit, he was talking to that lil freak that works in there."

Their boy Dave was standing close by and heard their conversation so he decided to let Rob in on what he knew.

"Man I know who pushes that Challenger. It's that nigga Sincere from Kinsman County."

"What the fuck is that nigga doing hanging down here?" Rob asked with a screwed up face.

"I don't know big Bro but I can find out for you," Tone responded now with a screwed up look on his face.

"Yeah, you do that." Rob told him walking off to his car.

FOURTEEN

Tez had been staying out the way because he didn't feel like being bothered by anyone. He hasn't eaten in days, maybe even weeks. The last time he saw his family they pissed him the fuck off. Now he sat in a small one bedroom musty apartment all alone talking to himself.

"I am only sixteen years old so why do I have so many damn problems. I'm tired of standing in that muthafuckin' nigga shadows. Everything just has to be about Promise. Yeah he's mommy's first son but damn I'm her baby boy. It's like she worships the ground the nigga walks on. That nigga could never do any wrong. Promise has been selling dope since he was thirteen and she ain't said shit. But once she found out the nigga gave me a pack to sell her ass went crazy. And now he ain't gave me shit since. Now ain't that some shit! I can't eat but everybody else can. And that muthafuckin' Sincere, she acts like she birthed the nigga her damn self. He ain't shit but a muthafuckin cousin so why does she treat him better than me. And every time I look at that damn Divine I want to shoot that hoe straight in her damn head. Baby Doll my ass, they treat that bitch like she's the Queen of muthafuckin' Egypt. Fuck that hoe! Fuck all them pussy ass niggas. I'm about to be the next King of Kinsman County."

He pulled out a small baggie and dumped the contents on a spoon. He dropped a small amount of water on the contents then held the spoon over a flame. After the contents liquefied he took a needle and sucked the contents up into a syringe. He then put a belt around his arm.

"And Innocence ain't shit but a lying bitch. She thinks I don't know her secret but yeah I know. Promise, what the fuck is a Promise? She got five damn kids four of our names begin with a D after our father. So where the fuck did she get the name Promise from? I know everybody has to wonder about that shit. But ain't anyone going to say shit to Ms. Innocence. To their asses she's so fuckin' perfect. If only they knew she's a fuckin' snake just like her oldest son."

He pulled the belt tight around his arm and pumped his fist for a vein to surface. Once he saw the vein he stuck the needle in his arm then pushed the contents of the needle into his blood stream. He closed his eyes and leaned his head back enjoying his first blast of heroin for the day going through his body.

"I hope she dies in that fuckin' hospital," was the last thing he said before he nodded out.

FIFTEEN

It's been an entire four weeks since Divine's first doctor's appointment when she found out she was indeed pregnant. And now she had to get up and get on her way to her second appointment. This once a month thing was going to get on her nerves.

She waited a little while longer to see if Promise was coming home since he didn't come home last night and he knew she had an appointment. He actually hadn't been spending his nights at home for about the past three weeks. But she could kind of understand why. Her being pregnant by someone else couldn't have been easy for him and then Innocence had slipped into a coma about two weeks ago. And they weren't any closer to finding out who did it and why. She knew he had the weight of the world on his shoulders.

She put on her shoes and tried his phone for the last time. He didn't answer so she left to go get the first look at her baby by herself.

❊❊❊❊❊❊❊

Promise looked at his phone seeing that Divine was calling him again. He knew why she was calling. Today was her second appointment and the doctor wanted to do an ultrasound so he could see exactly how far along she was. He wanted to be there for her but he just couldn't. He knew he told her he would be there for her no matter what. He said he would be at every appointment and for the birth, and that he didn't care who the father was. Because as long as the baby had her blood running threw his or her veins, that baby also belonged to him.

So why was he here with Carmen trying to keep his mind off Divine? He had actually sat outside their building all night debating if he should go in or not. Then at 8:00 sharp he made his way to 143rd. He knew he was wrong, dead wrong, but she was wrong for laying and fucking another nigga. He didn't care if she wasn't his woman yet. She had to know that she belonged to him. Telling himself fuck it, he grabbed Carmen by the back of her head pushing her down so she could suck his pains away.

⬥⬥⬥⬥⬥⬥⬥

Divine sat inside the doctor's office still trying to reach Promise. She was hoping he was just tied up and would make it there with her. She thought she should call Sincere to make sure everything was cool but decided against it. If something was wrong with Promise or anyone with the Fam her phone would have already been ringing. Whatever was going on with Promise was his own personal thing so nobody would know where he was. And it really didn't matter anyway because she knew exactly where he was she just didn't want to believe it.

"Ms. Dawson, Doctor Frazier will see you now. She also wants you to know that she's going to sit with you while the tech does your ultrasound. She wants to make sure that everything is okay with the baby for herself."

Divine gathered her things put her phone on silent and followed the medical assistant to the ultrasound room.

Dr. Frazier gave Divine a hug, "Good morning Divine, it's nice to see you today."

"Good morning Doc, how have you been?" She asked while returning the hug

"I should be asking you that. Has the spotting stopped? He's been gentle right?"

She smiled at her doctor. She was one of nicest people she had ever met and she has been her doctor since she had gotten her first female checkup at 13. "Yes, the spotting stopped. To tell you the truth he's scared now, so we haven't been having sex at all."

"Well I did tell him it was okay if you guys did. I told him it actually helps the pregnancy. Speaking of, where is he? I just knew he wouldn't miss this moment."

"His father has been admitted into the hospital so he's not going to make it. But he told me to come because he didn't want me missing any appointments," Divine responded lying straight through her teeth.

"I'm sorry to hear about his dad so let's hurry. I know you want to be there for him."

She left the doctor's office overjoyed. She was exactly nineteen weeks pregnant and was having a healthy baby boy. When she first found out that she was pregnant a month ago she was in denial. But seeing her beautiful baby on that screen changed everything. Now she was excited about being pregnant. And she wasn't going to let anything take her joy away. Not even Promise. Either he was going to deal or he wasn't.

Her first stop would be to see her mother. She couldn't wait to tell her she was about to be a grandmother.

But first she was going to try and call Promise one more time to let him know they were having a son.

She listened to his phone ring waiting for him to answer.

"Hello" a female voice answered.

She paused and looked at her screen because there was no way a hoe was answering Promise's phone. She put the phone back to her ear because sure enough she had the correct number.

"Um Hello" the female voice said again.

She smiled to herself thinking *no, the fuck he didn't*. She knew exactly who the female was. It was the corny hoe Carmen holding their dope on 143rd. "Yeah put Donnie on the phone."

"He's sleeping right now. Can I ask who's calling so I can have him call back you when he wakes up?"

Divine chuckled once again "Nawl, there's no need for all that lil mama. I'll get up with him later."

She closed her phone feeling the ice running threw her veins. She sat there in the parking lot with her mind all over the place. *Who the fuck did Promise think he was?*

Did he realize who he was fucking with? Maybe he didn't know her so well after all because if he did he wouldn't have pulled that bullshit. She tried to be understanding with their situation and his feelings. But for him now disrespecting her and fucking with her feelings wasn't part of the game. He knows she doesn't do betrayal. Yeah she knew he still fucked bitches and yeah she knew exactly where he was when she called. But to have her answer his phone like she was his main and Divine was the toy on the side was out of the question. And she knew he's probably asleep not knowing the hoe even answered his phone. But that's still his fault for not having his hoes in check. If he didn't want to be there for her that's all he had to say. She would have understood that. But he chose to sell her this dream of him accepting her child. He chose to tell her he was going to be there no matter what. Now he stood next to her father at the top of her betrayal list.

She opened her phone to make another call.

"What the hell is up with you? Didn't I tell your ass to get at me when I was at yo' mama's house? That was over a month ago."

"Well damn, I've been a little busy. I've had a lot going on." She replied a little caught off guard by the way he was speaking to her.

"Like what?"

"I'll tell you when I see you. It's about that time, where you at?"

"Where you think? On my way home so I can take of that. And yo' ass better show up!"

She looked at her phone seeing that he hung up on her. She thought *I think I'm kind of turned on a little. He has never talked to me like that.*

SIXTEEN

Pulling in the driveway she noticed she beat him there and figured she'd take advantage of that. She walked to the door and let herself in with her key. *He knew every move I made my ass* she thought to herself. Once in the house she took the quickest shower she could and hopped in the bed.

When he walked into the house a thousand and one things went through his mind. He has been so fucking stressed out because he felt like muthafuckas were watching him. And him not seeing her after he told her he needed to holla at her had him bugged out. But once he walked into his bedroom and saw her lying across the bed playing with her pussy he couldn't remember what the fuck he was mad at her about.

"Don't just stand there staring, get over here and eat my pussy."

"I think I'm going to watch."

Spreading her legs wide holding her pussy open she spoke very firmly. "I don't believe I stuttered. Now get over here and eat my pussy."

He stood there watching her and smiling. She loved to run shit. She had the biggest ego he has ever seen. He always let her have her way because that shit turned him on. But not today, he told her over a month ago he needed to talk to her and she didn't attempt to get at him. And what the fuck was up with her stomach he thought, frowning up his face.

She saw the look on his face and knew what he just noticed. While continuing to play with herself she told him, "No your eyes aren't deceiving you. We're nineteen weeks pregnant which means in a week we will be five months. And we're having a baby boy. Now can you please come eat this fat, hot, pregnant pussy?"

He couldn't believe his ears he was about to be a father. And by the only person in the world that he wanted to carry his child.

He pulled his clothes off then climbed into the bed on top of her. He stared down at her looking deep in her eyes. Even though they were just friends she was his heart. He would do any and everything for her. All she had to do was ask.

He leaned down to kiss her lips but she turned her head.

She didn't allow anyone to ever kiss her. No matter how bad she wanted to taste his juicy lips. Kissing was too personal and they were only friends. The day she and Promise kissed was her first time in all her twenty one years on earth.

He cupped her chin and turned her face back to his. She wasn't getting away with that shit today. She was carrying his child, she was his now.

He pressed his lips against hers but she didn't respond.

Looking at him like she was ready to kill, she slowly emphasized, "I'm telling you now if you force something on me that I don't want I promise you when it's over you will regret you ever knew me. I told you to eat my pussy not to kiss me. I don't kiss. You of all people should have figured that out by now. Now I'm going to tell you one last time. Eat my pussy or get the fuck off of me so I can go."

He looked down at her and knew if he didn't do as she asked she would get up and leave. And that was the last thing he wanted her to do. He had missed her something terrible. He just wished their relationship could be different. He let her have her way so much so how he could try to switch things up now. He would give her what she wanted once again hoping he didn't fuck up his chance to get him some pussy because she was good at getting her pussy ate and bouncing.

He did as he was told and slid down her body so he could be face to face with the fattest, juiciest pussy he had ever seen. He spread her fat lips and admired her clit. Her pussy was so damn fat that it swallowed her clit and if you wanted to taste her cream you had to put in some serious work to get it. And he was ready. He started eating her pussy the way he knew she liked it but he wasn't getting the responses that he was used to.

She tried to relax and get her nut but something just wasn't right. Usually her telling him what to do when to lick when to suck pushing his head in making him eat her how she wanted turned her on. That's how she really got her nut off by being demanding. But for some reason it wasn't working that day. Thinking, *that God-damn Promise, shit!*

She pushed his head away, "You know what, just stop. I can't get into it."

He looked up at her from between her big thighs pleading, "Why not? What's wrong? Give me another chance I promise I will get it right this time. Just tell me exactly what you want."

"I can't, I just can't. I think it's the pregnancy, maybe another time." She only told him that so his feelings wouldn't be hurt. But what she really couldn't understand was how he could be so hard in the streets. He Dogged niggas and bitches too for that matter, she had been a witness to how far his gangster could go. But when it came to her he tucked his tail and went to find somewhere to go hide. But then again it really didn't matter because if he tried to be any other way with her she would cut his ass off.

She didn't even have any conversation for him. She just rolled over to get her some much needed sleep.

She was awakened with him sitting next to her stroking his hand up and down her arm. When she opened her eyes he was staring into her face, "Come on let's go get in the tub."

She sat up and got out of bed following him to the master bathroom. Closing her eyes welcoming the warm water she eased down into the Jacuzzi tub.

Once she was comfortable he eased in behind her and wrapped his arms around her. He then kissed the side of her head.

"So tell me, when did you find out we were pregnant since you're almost five months?"

"I found out when I went to the doctor a month ago. My body was still spotting every month like a period so she recommended that I have an ultrasound done on my next scheduled visit. That was today and that's how I found out how far along I was."

"You've known you were carrying my baby for the last month and ain't said shit?"

"Yes, but I was in denial. Shit we always used a condom so I guess I just had to come to grips with that shit didn't work."

"Well if it means anything to you I'm glad you're carrying my child. I wouldn't want anyone but you raising my baby. Let me know when the next appointment is because I will be attending them all. Okay."

"Okay"

"Do you have the ultrasound pictures with you?"

"Yeah, I'll show them to you when we get out."

"Alright"

They sat there in silence for a while with her being in deep thought. *How could Promise betray me like that? He knew I didn't let anybody in my heart. He knew I didn't let anyone have any say in my life. Hell he knows everything about me, all my secrets. He was my first real relationship and I only gave him that chance because he knew me so well. Why would he fuck up? He's been making me know the entire time we were cool that he was the one for me. Well it doesn't matter anymore. Now he was going to be treated like the rest. We weren't even official for three months yet. And the real fucked up part about it is my damn body is betraying me also. I can't even get my pussy ate. What the fuck is that all about?*

"What's on your mind? Talk to me," he said while rubbing her arms.

"Nothing at all"

"Are you sure?"

"Yup"

"Well when I told yo' ass to get at me I was trying to take you out of town with me. But you so damn hard headed. Next time I tell you to do something you make sure you do it," he said as he pushed her head to the side.

Pushing her back into him, "Boy whatever and you better keep your hands to yourself."

"Girl you better go on but real talk, a nigga been missing you like crazy. I know I don't discuss my business with you but I've been going through some shit. I've got this eerie feeling like somebody has been watching me. And I don't think it's the police. There is some nigga from Kinsman I've never seen on Cedar before been hanging around there. My brother said he be talking to some hoe at the Urban store but I don't trust the shit."

Her ears perked up. "Why do you care if a nigga hanging on Cedar?"

"That's where I get my money."

This time she sat up and turned to get a look at his face. "What do mean that's where you get your money? You're always on Hough so that's where I thought you did your business. I didn't even know you still hung on Cedar."

"I supply Hough and that's where I kick it most of the time but my grounds is Cedar, that's all me."

She sat back shocked. All that time she thought Rob ran Hough. Yeah he was from Cedar but every time she talked to him his ass was over in Hough Heights. Damn, was she that disconnected from her own hood that she didn't know she was about to take over her own nigga's spot. "Fuck" was all she could say.

"Fuck what?"

"Nothing just thinking to myself."

"Oh yeah, my brother ran into Jay. He told my brother he wanted to eat so I'm letting him get that money. For the lil muthafucka to be only sixteen he hustles his ass off. I don't think he ever sleeps."

Fuck, Fuck, Fuck and my brother getting money down there too. Fuck! Was all she could say, "Well that's good. He's eating."

"Do you want his number so you can give him a call? He told me he hasn't seen you in a while."

"Nawl, there's no need. I'll bump heads with him sooner or later."

"Why wouldn't you want your brother's number Dee? You know you're one cold hearted female. But um can I ask you a personal question?"

"Depends on how personal."

"What's happened in your life that you won't allow anyone to love you?"

She closed her eyes and leaned her head back into his chest, "Nothing has happened to me. It's just the ones you think love you are the same ones that betray you. Now

I don't want to say anything else about it. So just leave it alone!"

After finishing her bath she left to go call off her dogs.

SEVENTEEN

Sincere sat on his Italian leather sofa enjoying his purple haze and listening to his favorite artist, Al Green. His eyes wandered around his apartment and he liked what he saw. Everything was good for him right now, except for one thing. He missed his Aunt Innocence.

His mind floated to another place as he thought about his life.

His mother had been murdered when he was only five years old. That wasn't enough time for him to really know or remember her. His Aunt Innocence would tell him a different story about his mother every week. Every Sunday when he went to his aunt's house they would cook and eat breakfast together. When they were finished eating she would sit on the couch and he would lay his head in her lap. Innocence would rub his head and tell him about an adventure she and his mother had when they were growing up. It had been their little thing ever since his mother passed.

Innocence did everything she could to try and help him remember her best friend, Simone Mitchell. She took him in after his mother was murdered, which was before she had any children of her own. She raised him as her nephew and her children's cousin. None of her children knew they weren't blood cousins except for Sincere and Promise. She couldn't hold the truth from them. Their relationship with her was too solid for her to feed those two lies. When he asked about his father she couldn't give him any answers. His mother actually had him when they were only fourteen years old and Innocence never meet the older cat Simone was sneaking out to see. The only thing she could tell him was that he was some kind of pimp from Central and she thought he was responsible for his Simone's death.

When Sincere became of an age where he felt he could take a man's life he went on Central asking questions about a pimp from back in the day, but no one had any answers for him. He went on this mission for years. Going around talking to old heads and street people but he never had any luck. He just chalked it up to the idea that the guy probably lied to his mother about who he really was and what he did. So now he felt he would never be able to revenge his mother's death.

He decided he needed to put his blunt out because it was taking his mind places he didn't want to revisit at that moment. All he knew was Innocence needed to wake her ass up and get the hell out of that hospital. He was missing his Aunt like crazy. She was his passage to the first woman he had ever loved but didn't know.

He stood up from the couch and went to his mantel to look at the only picture he had of his mother. It was a picture of her and his aunt at Lake Erie beach. He smiled at the picture because at the time she was pregnant with him. He couldn't believe how small she was kicking it with his big ass in her stomach. As he looked at the picture he could see himself in his mother but also he knew that a lot of his features must have come from the man he wanted dead. He gave the picture a kiss and decided it was time for him to get out of the house before he lost his mind.

He really didn't have shit to do so he thought he would get up with the friend he's been spending time with and see what she was up to.

When Cherokee heard the ring tone *Oh nana, what's my name* by Rihanna, she knew it was Sincere.

She answered "Yes Sincere".

"You're saying that like I'm bothering you or something."

"I didn't mean for it to sound that way because you're definitely not bothering me. I'm just a little aggravated right now. But what's going on?"

"Nothing with me, I'm just trying to see you. Now why are you aggravated?"

Crossing her legs while looking through a magazine she replied, "My car was acting up on me this morning so I had to bring it to the shop. They're trying to tell me a damn water pump is going to cost me five hundred dollars. But I'm mad because now that I got the car here I have to have them fix it because it ain't doing shit."

"What shop you at?" He asked while putting on his shoes.

"Some father and son shop over here on 153rd and Harvard."

"I know whose spot that is. Tell them I said don't touch your damn car. I'm on my way. I'm going to have your car towed to the spot where I take mine to."

"Okay, that's fine but will it be ready by tomorrow? I have to get back to work on Monday."

"Don't worry about all that I got you," and with that said he hung up the phone.

She looked at her phone "Damn, okay then."

After he got her car situated at his shop he decided they would take a trip to Beachwood mall. He was stepping out that night and needed something to wear.

He glanced over at her and really admired her style. She was a little bitty something compared to him. She was only about 5' even and wasn't no more than 115 pounds. She had a pretty brown complexion with a bean shaped head that was full of long hair that she kept in a long layered bouncy wrap. And she had a pair of beautiful shaped eyes that he seemed to get lost in when he looked at her. What he liked most though was her smile with those big juicy lips. He loved kissing her, something that he never really did. And her one slightly bow-leg drove him crazy when she walked in front of him. He couldn't wait to pin her little ass up against a wall.

He reached across and rubbed his fingers through her hair. It felt so soft and pretty to him. "Is this all you ma?"

"Um yeah, why would you ask me that?"

"Just wanted to know, I really don't care for that weave shit. But um where my lil lady at, I got her gift? I called you the other day so I could drop it off but you didn't answer." he explained to her as he parked the car and glanced over at her.

"I saw your missed call later on that night. When I got off work I was tired so I took a nap but I wound up asleep for most of the night. I didn't want to call you back that late."

"Why? I'm not a baby."

"I know that. But I didn't know if you were busy or something so I just didn't call. I knew if you really wanted something you would have called back."

"Yeah I hear you talking Miss Cherokee. Let's get in this mall so we can get this shit over with. I hate shopping."

Walking back to the car behind Sincere with her hands full of bags Cherokee couldn't help but look at him in amazement. She loved his long sexy bow-legs. His walk was so smooth and sexy with a little bop to it. Walking beside him in the mall made her feel like a midget compared to his 6'4" and his 222lbs. She loved when he would walk up behind her wrap his arms around her and bend down to rest his chin on the top of her head. His skin was like dark chocolate and she couldn't wait to get a taste. And his smile, wow he had the prettiest set of perfect white teeth. She loved the way his big juicy lips felt on hers. And she knew he had a big ass dick and couldn't wait to take that ride. *Damn I think I'm about to cum on myself just looking and thinking about him.*

He popped his trunk and placed their bags inside. They hopped in his cherry red Challenger and were on their way to her spot.

He had bought her and her daughter just as much shit as he bought himself. Which was odd for him because he had never bought a female anything besides his aunt little cousins and Divine. Shit he had never been in a real relationship which would give him the opportunity to do for a female. He did what he had to do with hoes then he went on about his way. He never wanted to get too close to a female letting them into his world. His world was dark and ugly. Not too many women could handle what he went through day in and day out. Not to mention the possibility of jail. He for sure wasn't going to be all in love and have to leave his bitch behind for some other nigga. And he couldn't handle the thought of her getting lost in his ugly world and coming up missing or dead. Hell no! That's the shit that happened to his mother. Nope having a main wasn't worth all that. Unless she was tuff as nails like Divine. And there just weren't too many bitches out there like her. She was a breed all of her own. He guessed it was from her hanging around niggas all of her life.

His phone rang taking him out of his trance. "What's up Twin? I just had you on my mind."

"Nothing much, tired of this pregnant shit though. I'm so fucking emotional I don't know what the fuck to do. I mean like shit that wouldn't even bother me is making me shed a thousand tears. Sin, this shit ain't right. I can't wait to drop this load."

"I'm sorry Doll, what got you going crazy now?"

"Yo' boy Promise. Why the fuck did we even cross the line? Sin, we were good. Why that nigga have to take me there? He hasn't called or even tried to check up on me. Even on some I'm his nigga shit. Damn we are best friends and now he doesn't even care about me or my seed. Twin that shit is so fucked up. I mean it's like we were never cool, friends, crime partners, hell even fucking roommates. His money is my money, my money is his money and this is how he wants to treat me? But it's cool. I got something for his ass. His feelings go' be real hurt when I get finished with this emotional shit and show him my true colors. He thinks shit sweet because I'm kind of on a vacation right now." Divine raved into the phone while running out of breath.

"Come on now Doll you know that nigga love the fuck out of you. He just going through something right now. So please don't start any of that tit for tat bullshit because on the real we both know that nigga can get real retarded when it comes to you. So please don't do no dumb shit like fucking around with some other nigga. All that's gone do is put another murder under Promise's belt. And if yo' ass is doing something now you need to watch your surroundings. That nigga might be going through something and you might think he ain't thinking about you but you know he ain't going to let go of that leash he got you on that easily. He's just giving you a little room to wiggle right now. Alright? Oh yeah you know he's questioning why that one move was put off."

"Yeah whatever, tell him because I said so. Now what are you doing I'm hungry?"

"Just left the mall, I'm on my way to my little friend's house." He answered while glancing over at Cherokee. "Do you want me to bring you something to eat?"

"Hell nawl, not if you wit' yo little boo. A female got my twin at the mall, I got to meet her. And nigga I know you got me something too?"

"You go' meet her real soon. And you know good and well I got you something and I looked out for my nephew."

"Thanks Twin, I love you. And have fun with your Boo."

Looking shocked and laughing he replied, "Yeah you're right you need to hurry up and drop that load. My nephew got you saying I love you and shit."

"Fuck you Sin!" Divine yelled into her phone

"I love you too Baby Doll, but please be careful. We're already going through enough family drama. We don't need to add some more bullshit. You feel me?"

"Yes I do and bye boy!"

He hung up the phone smiling and thinking that damn crazy ass Baby Doll was his heart.

Thinking of how sexy Sincere was Cherokee turned in her seat and to get a good look at him. Yeah he looked good but she didn't think the look would look that well on a female. "I didn't know you were a twin."

"Not a real twin, we just say we're twins because we share the same birth date but different years. I'm exactly one year older than her. We are best friends though and I do love her like she's my sister."

The crazy part was some people actually thought they were twins because they were so close to each other and did favor a pinch especially in their eyes.

Sincere looked ahead thinking how he was just so comfortable around Cherokee to be telling her his business. There was something about her that made him want to feel closer to her.

"Oh okay that's cool. But Babe look, you're about to pass my street."

"I wasn't even paying attention, my mind was somewhere else." He responded as he turned left on 125th and Kinsman down her street.

EIGHTEEN

Promise sat in an office at Hanna's Realty Company going over the final paper work for his new house. He couldn't dare go back to that condo with Divine there going in and out. The last time he was there it felt as if the walls were literally closing in on him. He had to get out of there. He needed a fresh start with his new life. So much was changing for him. Now he was thinking that after he finished with his paper work he needed to go to the furniture store. He didn't like doing all this on his own. He could really use Divine's help right now. But then again he thought he did a damn good job of picking out the house so furniture should be a piece of cake.

After he finished with the furniture store he decided to go see his mother.

When he entered his mother's room he gave his Uncle Freaky some dap and his mother a kiss on the forehead. He sat down in the chair next to her bed and laid his head on the edge of the bed.

"Damn Nephew you look like you're going through Hell."

"Nawl not Hell Unc, remember that's where I'm from and what I bring. But I am going through some shit though."

"Do you want to talk about it?" His uncle asked pulling up a chair to sit next to him.

"I'm good Freaky you know that sharing shit ain't for me."

"Yeah I know. Well you just missed Sincere and Baby Doll. They sat up here chilling with Innocence for about two hours. Baby Doll is wearing her pregnancy real good too."

"That's good." Promise responded not really caring to hear about Divine right now.

"You do know that you're not going to be able to dodge her forever?"

"Yeah I know. I just got to do me right now. I have a lot of things to take care of."

"As long as you know and don't fuck around and take too long. Divine is a good girl any man would be jumping to have her on his arm."

Sitting up in his chair and leaning his head back, "They won't be doing shit but digging their own graves fucking with mines. And besides can't nobody tame her ass but me."

"Boy you're something else. But what's good with the leads on my sis in law right here?"

"I'm going to keep it all the way real wit you Unc. I think yo' brother and yo' youngest nephew got something to do with this, more so your nephew."

Freaky looked at his nephew like he had lost his mind. "Promise what the hell are you talking about? My brother wouldn't do shit to hurt yo' momma and damn sure not Tez."

"You might be right. But right now that's how it's looking. When I get all my info together I'll let you know."

"Why Divine and Sincere ain't said shit to me. They were here for two damn hours?"

"That's because I haven't told them yet. If it's true I don't want to put that burden on them. Tez is my blood and I will handle it."

"And my brother, who's going to handle him?" Freaky asked looking at his favorite nephew.

"Since I'm being honest today you and I both know that man's blood isn't running through my veins. I'll see how Innocence wants to handle that when she gets her ass up. But if she doesn't wake up I'm going to personally send him to Hell with my real daddy."

NINETEEN

Sincere had been spending a lot of time with Cherokee since Divine had finally met her and gave him the okay. Her approval meant a lot to him because he knew she could smell a nothing ass hoe from a mile away. Especially when it came to him sometimes when they went out and a female would approach him he would just look over to her to see what her facial expression was. By seeing his twin's face he knew if he should just walk away or get the number so he could fuck every now and then. He never got the thumbs up look until she met Cherokee which really meant a lot to him.

He sat in the back parking lot of Key Bank waiting for Cherokee to get off work. He had gotten her car out of the shop but he enjoyed taking her to and from work. It was a Saturday which meant she was getting off at one o'clock then they were going to get her baby girl and take her to the park. He loved her little girl like she was his very own. She told him her daughter's father was never a part of her life. He didn't care if her daddy saw her or not but that was one of the very reasons why he spent so much time with her. Every little girl deserved to have a good male figure in their life.

He looked up and saw Cherokee walking to his car. She looked sexier than ever in a white ruffled blouse unbuttoned far enough to show off just a little bit of her cleavage, a black A-line skirt, some black three and a half inch peep-toe Guess pumps with a gold heel and a red and gold Guess bucket purse. When she got in the car she leaned over and gave him a juicy kiss on his lips.

"Damn Bay, where that come from?"

Cupping his face and kissing him some more, "Just happy to see you you've been on my mind all day."

Pulling out of the parking lot and riding down 140th he glanced over at her and saw something he hasn't seen in her before. "You sure you're just happy to see me or is something else going on with you?"

Yeah something was going on with her alright. She'd been hanging around his sexy ass day and night for the past couple of months and she was tired of the good girl act. It was time for her to Sin. She reached her hand across the seat to grab his hand so she could let him feel exactly what was going on with her. She pulled her skirt up and opened her legs guiding his hands inside of her panties.

Playing in her pussy, "God-damn Kee, you wet as fuck."

"Mmmmm, I told you you've been on my mind all day." She hummed with her eyes closed enjoying the feeling he was giving her.

Driving and playing with her pussy he asked, "My place or yours?"

She placed her hand on top of his so she could push his fingers on her clit to feel more pressure. She rotated her hips ready to explode, "Yours Babe, you got me all to yourself for the rest of the day and all night long."

"Where's my baby girl?"

"With her grandmother, we don't have to pick her up until tomorrow evening."

"That's what's up." He told her as he pulled into his Aunt's driveway. He couldn't wait until he got to his place he needed to make her cum now. He reached and pulled her over on his lap so she could straddle him. She instantly started grinding on his crouch and tonguing him down. He pulled her panties to the side and slipped his first two fingers inside her pussy fucking her as if it was his dick.

"Oh... yes... Sincere... fuck me baby. Um... fuck me." She rode his hand like she was in a rodeo show.

Kissing her on the side of her neck he whispered in her ear, "Kee your pussy is so... fucking wet. Can she get wetter for me baby?"

She started grinding on his fingers even harder. He was making her feel so fucking good. "Yes Sin, yes... you ready baby?"

Biting her shoulder he moaned, "Give it to me Cherokee let me see what you got baby."

Him biting her shoulder drove her crazy. She started bucking all over his hand grabbing his head and smothering his face in her chest. She was cumming so hard and it seemed she wasn't stopping any time soon.

"Uh...uh...oh...Mmm...Yes...Sincere... God yes."

When her body stopped trembling she started laughing on the side of his neck. "I can't believe I just came that hard. That's been building up inside of me for months."

He smacked her on her ass. "Get yo' ass over there, I'm about to take you home and fuck the shit out of yo' little ass."

She didn't move to the side, she kept grinding her pussy on his crouch. "No Sin, I want some dick now. I'm ready to feel you inside of me."

He pulled out his dick thrusting it inside of her letting her get a feel of what was yet to come.

She was so surprised by the girth and length of his dick that she actually tried to climb off of it.

He pulled her back down and held her in place with his dick buried deep inside her. "Where you think you going? You said you wanted to feel, so now feel."

She didn't know what else to do but accept the pain. She knew his dick was going to be big but his shit was ridiculous. She attempted to slow ride him but he stopped her. He put his hand behind her head and kissed her juicy lips with his dick still deep inside.

"Kee, I don't think you know how good this pussy feels on my dick. I hope you know what you're getting yourself into. I'm not going to play bullshit games with you, it's not my style. You keep it all the way one hundred with me and I'll keep it one hundred with you. So if this is something we're going to do we're going to do it right. That shit with you not answering yo' phone stops. And all that laughing and giggling shit you do in nigga's faces when they try to holla at you stops. Only ego you need to feed is mine. And when I call you better muthafuckin' come running, do you understand me?"

He lifted her head from his shoulders so he could get a good look at her face. Looking like she was lost in ecstasy she nodded her head up and down real slow.

"I don't know what that means. Now do you understand me?"

"Yes Sincere, I understand you."

"Are you sure this is what you want?"

"Yes Sincere."

He lifted her off his dick and smacked her ass again. He pulled out of his Aunt's yard and was on his way to get him some much needed pussy. She had his dick so hard it felt like it was about to break.

As soon as he closed his door Sincere picked Cherokee up and threw her against the wall. He snatched open the front of his pants letting them fall to the floor and pulled his dick out of his boxers.

She couldn't take the waiting, "Babe come on, I---, Oww... Yes...!"

He rammed his dick inside her, "Shut yo' ass up, don't rush me wit' mines. I've wanted to put yo' ass on this wall since the first day I saw you.

"Yes... fuck me Sincere.... please fuck me.....this dick feels so good Babe, yes...."

He steadied his feet, grabbed her waist and guided her up and down his dick with long deep strokes.

"Yes, just like that, just like that. Shit Sincere, my pussy is about to cum...Fuck...Sincere Babe...I'm cumming...yes...

"Cum on this dick." He started fucking her even harder. "Cum on this dick, damn…. Kee," he hollered cumming along with her.

He held her there up against the wall with his dick still inside her and with her legs wrapped around him. He kissed her neck, her cheek, and then her juicy lips. They stayed that way for about another five minutes.

"Babe, I don't even know what to say." Cherokee finally spoke as she rubbed his head.

Carrying her to the bedroom, "There ain't shit to say but I got you now."

And Sincere did exactly what she said. He fucked her for the rest of the day and all night long.

TWENTY

Divine had finally reached her ninth month of pregnancy. Dr. Frazier told her she was 36 weeks and now she needed an appointment once a week. Once a month got on her nerves so she damn sure didn't want to go once a week. And Rob was a man true to his word. Ever since she told him about the baby he went to every appointment with her. They had been spending a lot of time together. She was so thankful for him during this time in her life.

She was never the one that needed to be around anyone for long periods of time. She was her mother's only child so she was used to being by herself. Even though she and Promise were close and lived together they didn't spend every waking moment with each other. He did his thing and she did hers. Most of their time together was at night when they were relaxing in bed. He wasn't the type to like to go out to eat, or to the movies, or even out of town on trips. He was a hood nigga all day every day. She used to joke with him telling him if anyone wanted to find him all they had to do was ride through the 40's on Kinsman. All he would say was, when they come looking they're going to have a rude awakening. And he was right because he didn't have a problem with sending anyone to their maker.

She and Sincere were actually closer than her and Promise. She guessed probably because they were around the same age. Sincere was her movie and out to eat partner. They would hop in the car for a road trip at any given moment. And even though she didn't express herself a lot Sincere would be the one she called when she needed to vent. Their pretend twin bond was unbreakable. But now he had himself a Boo so she didn't have anyone to kick it with. Even though Sincere said he would cut his time short with his girl for her she would never take that away from him. She was happy he had a girl he could spend quality time with besides her and Innocence.

By her needing so much companionship with the pregnancy, that's where Rob filled the void. He found something for them to do every day, even if it was as simple as going to a museum. He did any and everything to keep her happy. He didn't want her to stress about anything while she was carrying his child. And he was okay with spending all his time with her without any sex. He just figured after the baby came she would be back to her normal bossy self.

He actually didn't know about the other life she lived. He had no clue about her Kinsman County life. He just knew she had a bunch of guy cousins she liked to hang around. He damned sure didn't know about her and Promise. To him he was her one and only lover and he prayed that one day she would let him in her heart to be her only love also. That's why he would do whatever he could to keep niggas out of her path.

After their doctor's appointment the two went to Border's Express in Tower City to get her some books. She was dying to read Keisha Ervin's book, *Gunz and Roses*.

She loved her urban fiction novels. She read like two books a week.

Even though she loved to read urban books she also had a fetish for vampires so once she read the *Vampire Huntress* series by L.A. Banks she was now hooked on paranormal romances. After picking out her books she was in a rush to go back to Rob's house so she could crack open the second book in Larissa Ione's Demonica series *Desire Unchained*. She was so excited she started reading in the car.

Once they made it to the house she flew inside took a quick shower and jumped into bed to finish reading. By the time she made it to the 12th chapter she was in love with the main charter, Shade. He reminded her so much of Promise. He was so aggressive and protective yet loving at the same time. And now reading the book only made her hot and horny thinking of her Don. She didn't care for the feeling seeing as though it wasn't shit she could do about it so she closed the book so she could get some sleep. Rob covered her up and kissed her on the forehead as she drifted off to sleep thinking of Promise.

❧❧❧❧❧

Sincere walked inside of Whitmore's and saw Promise sitting in his usual seat. He stepped up to him at the bar thinking, enough is enough. He was tired of his cousin looking like he lost his best friend. Well technically he did but damn he didn't have to let the world know. Promise was one of the strongest niggas he knew. That's why he couldn't understand why he was taking this Divine shit so bad. She wasn't going anywhere. Sincere and everyone else knew her heart belonged to Promise.

He leaned over and spoke to Promise in his ear. "What's up my nigga? You're over here looking real bad."

"Fuck you! I'm cool."

"Are you sure? You look like you haven't had any sleep in months."

Throwing his third shot back. "Yeah I'm sure. Ain't had time to sleep, been taking care of a lot of business."

Sincere signaled the waitress so he could order himself a drink. "You sure that's what it is?"

"Yeah I'm sure. But um since you're here, why don't you round up some of the Fam for me. I need to go take care of some personal business."

TWENTY ONE

Divine could feel a presence standing over her so she eased her hand under the pillow for her gun.

"It's not there. And I see you sleep real comfortable with this nigga, huh!"

From the other side of the bed she heard, "If you move I will blow your fuckin' brains out."

She opened her eyes slowly and saw Promise standing over her with his 9mm with the silencer attached in one hand and her baby nine in the other. As she sat up in the bed he tucked her gun into the waist of his pants. Once she got comfortable with her back against the headboard she looked over at Sincere as he stood over Rob with his gun to Rob's head. Rob laid there with his eyes wide open looking at her like what the fuck is going on.

She stared at Promise in his eyes and saw nothing but hurt and death. She could understand the death part but why the fuck was he looking at her like she hurt his very soul. He was the one who told her he accepted her with the baby and then turned his back on her. He was the one who let his corny ass hoe answer his damn phone being disrespectful like she was the side line hoe. Now here this muthafucka stood disturbing her damn sleep and a good ass dream of her riding the fuck out of his dick. What part of the game is this? She gave him an evil smirk because she knew what he was there for. He wouldn't have found where she was, snuck into the house, and even brought Sincere along for no reason. Yeah she knew he didn't come all that way for nothing. She turned to fluff her pillow and laid her body back down on the bed. She pulled the sheet over herself and turned over on her side so that her back was to Promise and she was then facing Rob.

Promise let two go from his nine, "POP" "POP".

He sat down on the bed next to his Baby Doll. He rolled her over on her back and pulled the sheet down. He pulled her night shirt over her stomach and rubbed her stomach in full slow circles. He looked up at her face then bent down and gave loving kisses to her stomach. He pulled her shirt back down over her stomach and stood. He then pulled the sheet all the way down off of her body and reached out his hand.

"Come on. It's time for you to come home."

She sat up in the bed looking back at Rob. He lay there with his eyes still open with two bullet holes in his forehead. She stared at the blood oozing out of the holes sliding down his face.

"Get out yo' feelings and let's go." She heard Promise say with a little sympathy in his voice.

She turned her body to the side of the bed and reached out for his hand. She stood up in front of him. She searched his cold eyes and saw him for who he really was. She'd known him to murder many, but for a reason. What she saw now looking back at her was a heartless, non remorseful, sick killer.

He stroked the side of her face. "Baby Doll, this was bound to happen sooner or later. And I preferred sooner. I gave him a little time with his seed because he was the biological father and I knew you needed a lot of attention during this pregnancy that I wasn't able to provide. But you knew good and well I wasn't having no man walk this earth saying he's the real father of my son. I mean really, how long did you think I was going to let you play house with this nigga? Now get your heart off your sleeve and let's go!"

She slid her feet into her Uggs boots that he must have brought up the stairs with him and followed behind him.

He stopped at the door looking back at Sincere.

"Don't worry cousin. You know I got it. You just go and get yo' house back in order. That's goes for you too Doll. I already told you, we as a family don't need to be going through this unnecessary shit."

They both gave Sincere a head nod and walked out of Rob's bedroom door.

When they reached the hallway leading to the stairs she saw DeAndre, three of their soldiers, and three of their house cleaners and they all had their pistols in hand ready for war if need be. There were no words exchanged as she and Promise passed their goons on their way down the stairs and out of the door.

She stared out of the car window in a daze rubbing her stomach. She couldn't believe Rob was gone. Normally she only had sympathetic feelings for her family and close people in her circle. But in a sense Rob was part of that circle. She had known him her entire life. They grew up together around the same neighborhoods. He wasn't her first love well he wasn't her love at all, but he considered to be her first. She had been having sex with him since she was seventeen. And he was the father of her child. He took care of her in his own way. Anything she wanted, Rob made sure he got it. He was one of the few that she trusted with her life. She even trusted him with her mother's and grandmother's lives also. She knew for sure he trusted her with his and she failed him. They just started spending real time together enjoying each other's company on another level. It wasn't just about sex any more. Actually they hadn't been sexually active since the day she conceived. She had just been spending quality time with him while keeping her mind off Promise and trying to stay stress free for her baby. She would have never wished death on him and especially not by the hands of Promise. True she knew what they had would have eventually had to come to an end, but not by death.

Promise drove quietly down highway 271 North stealing glances at Divine. He knew she was upset but what did she expect? She knew he wasn't going to let her play house too long with another man. And her ass had always known he wasn't playing with a full deck. Couldn't she give him a little credit for letting the nigga live as long as he did? He let the man have a little time with his child even though the baby was still in the womb. But now that she was in her ninth month of pregnancy that shit was over. It was now his time. She was his Queen and he was going to be the only father that the baby knew. As he looked at her he felt bad about missing most of her pregnancy. She looked so beautiful pregnant. Her skin was so clear and it seemed to even glow. Her stomach wasn't as big as he thought it would be but her ass sure was wide as hell. Thinking of her ass now gave him a fucked up vision in his head of that nigga hittin' it from the back.

When he pulled up in a driveway at a house on South Woodland Divine wondered whose house they were stopping at. All she wanted to do was go home and climb into bed and try to forget the night had ever happened.

He parked the car and sat silently for a couple of minutes. He shifted his body a little to get a good look at her. He took a deep breath asking with a heavy heart, "So you've been letting that nigga fuck my pussy and nut all on my baby?"

She couldn't believe her ears. Now she knew he was truly sick for sure. After murdering a man that's all his ass could think about was his fucking pussy.

"If it was so much of your pussy you wouldn't be asking me shit about it. You didn't want my pussy anymore remember. You weren't thinking about me so why the fuck do you care?" She responded sarcastically.

Before he could even realize what he was doing his hand was grabbed tightly around the back of her neck.

She stared him dead in the eyes, "This how we doing it now?"

He matched her stare then took his hand from around her neck. "I don't know why I'm tripping. I know you ain't let that nigga fuck. That's my heaven, she probably wouldn't even get wet for that muthafucka anyway." He opened his car door stepped out then slammed it. He walked around the car to the passenger side opened the door and told her, "Let's go".

Getting out of the car she thought how she couldn't stand his ass. She hated how he knew her and her body so well.

The house he took them to was so beautiful. She was in love wondering whose house it was.

When he reached the door and placed a key into the key hole she was beyond intrigued. They stepped inside the house and the alarm system started blaring. He stepped behind her to lock the door and then told her to go to the control panel. When she reached the panel he told her the code. She turned to look at him just to see him giving her a smile. The code was the same one they used at their condo. Once she silenced the alarm she felt his hands around her rubbing her stomach.

With his mouth pressed against her ear he whispered, "I apologize for putting my hands on you. I give you my word that shit will never happen again. I know how you feel about that shit but you also got to stop testing me. It's like you do and say shit just to see how far you can take me. But you should know by now I won't hurt you physically. I've got other ways to make you behave." At that moment he pinched both of her nipples making her squeal. "But I will kill every nigga around you if I have to."

She closed her eyes leaning her head back on his shoulder with tears sneaking down her face. "I know those aren't tears I see? Where they do that at? I've known you damn near 10 years and have never seen you cry, so please tell me you're not shedding tears for that nigga?" He asked while pinching her nipples even harder.

"Dontae, I would never disrespect you by crying for no man. These tears are for us. I don't understand how we went so wrong." She moved his hands from her nipples and guided them down to her stomach. "Don, we have been close for so long and we both know each other's limits. We had more respect for each other when we were best friends. So why when we became a couple it seems everything went wrong? I know my carrying another man's child was the main source of our problems. But Don, I asked you did you want to step away from the relationship, and you said no. You're the one that said you were going to be here for me when you didn't have to. We could have gone back to the way we were. But instead you ignored me and turned to someone else. You had the female answering your phone and everything."

He stopped rubbing her stomach, "Answering my phone, ain't no broad answer my phone."

"Yes she did Don, either way I'm over it. But on that day I felt so betrayed by you. Like I said we know each other's limits and you know betrayal is something I just don't do."

"Baby Doll I promise you I didn't know she answered my phone. And I'm going to handle that shit ASAP."

"Don, don't worry about it. I know you fuck outside of me. Shit I can tell you who, when, and how you fucked them. But let's not get too comfortable and get caught slipping again. And I would honestly say I'm speaking for the both of us. I know what I was doing was wrong. But Don this pregnancy has been one emotional roller coaster and I didn't like being alone. I needed that companionship for some odd reason."

"Divine, trust me when I tell you I know what you needed. I always have and I always will. But I couldn't give you all the attention and affection you required at the time. I was stressed from every angle. Doll, I haven't had a good night's sleep in I don't know how long. My mind was on my mom, my Queen, my money, and my son. I had to make sure my baby wasn't coming home from the hospital to a damn condo. My lil man deserves a big ass house with a big ass yard to play in. And I needed to make sure I had everything on the streets taken care of because I'm not leaving your side this last month of your pregnancy and the first couple of months after he's born. Did you honestly think you were getting away with something when you were with that nigga? I've always known where you were and what you were doing. And tonight I had to end all that bullshit. It was time for you to come home. So Baby I had to go hard and get our money right. My only problem now is Innocence pulling through."

He turned her around to face him so he could look into her eyes and bring her soul back home to him. "Divine Nanette, I apologize from the bottom of my heart for hurting you and it will never happen again. Even those who's, when's, and how's you were talking about. I don't need that shit. Trust when I tell you, you're more than enough to keep me happy and satisfied. Now come on so I can give you a tour of your new home."

Divine loved her new home. Promise had out done himself. He had gotten her one of those big ass houses with the manicured lawns she fantasized about on South Woodland. And out of that entire big ass house he had only furnished and decorated two of the rooms. He did their room and the baby's nursery. She didn't even have to ask him why because she already knew what his response would be. *Because that's my son and our bedroom is my domain, the rest of the house belongs to you.*

TWENTY TWO

Mad as hell at herself Divine pulled in the Pernel's funeral home parking lot on 71st and Cedar. She knew she should have arrived early. Rob's home going was packed. But before she could even get out of the car good Rob's lil brother Tone stepped to her with blood shot red eyes. He looked as if he had been crying all week.

"What's good Dee? Can I hop in real quick and holla at you?"

She didn't know where his head was so she made sure kept her trigger finger ready. "It's cool Tone, hop in."

Once he was in the car he sat there in silence for a couple of minutes trying to collect his thoughts.

"Dee, I want you to know no matter what your baby will be taken care of. My mother is dying to meet you. I'm pretty sure she's going to smother you and my nephew. But I want you to know that the niggas that took my brother's life are going to pay. I promise you that. I think I got a good idea who did this."

She cleared her throat and shifted in her seat. She knew her family would not have left any evidence. But could they have fucked up this one time?

Usually they didn't even leave a trace of the body but Sincere felt a certain way about disposing of their victim this time. When he got her alone he had a heart to heart with her. He told her he just couldn't do it because that was the real father of her baby and Rob deserved to be laid to rest properly by his family meaning also his baby. He stressed to her that the only thing Rob did wrong was get her pregnant. If she wasn't carrying his seed he would have still been alive. They had been fucking around for years and he had never done her dirty and always showed her respect. He also told her that she should attend the funeral because if she didn't it would just make their sister Karma angry. He knew Promise would have no understanding and wouldn't give a fuck about Karma's ass so he told her he would keep Promise busy while she went. If Promise knew she was there she probably would be getting buried along with Rob. But did Sincere having a heart for once fuck everything up for their family?

"So, who do think did this Tone?"

"That nigga Black peoples"

She had a look of confusion on her face. "What do you mean Black peoples? I know you're not talking about Black from Quincy? Why would they want to murder Rob?"

"I'm going to keep it all the way real wit you Dee. There is no point of lying to you anymore because now my brother is dead and gone. It really wasn't any point in lying to you in the first place. If he would have let you know how he felt about you a long time ago maybe this wouldn't have happened."

"Tone what the hell is you rambling on about? I don't understand why would Rob's feelings towards me have anything to do with Black?"

Tone closed his eyes and took a couple of deep breaths. "We both know you and Rob had y'all own little thing that no one knew of. It was cool because it was y'all thing. I don't know how deep it really went seeing as though y'all have been fucking for years and never made it official. But I do know my brother was deeply in love with you. When I say in love, I mean in love. That nigga had a thousand and one hoes. Most of them are in there right now. But in my brother's head you was his woman. Now Black was on our pay roll, getting good money too. But the nigga started getting greedy and started penny pinching which was a violation but he could have lived. But when Rob saw you and Black having breakfast and chopping it up real tough that nigga went ballistic. Trying to get at you was a major violation. So bottom line was Black had to go."

She couldn't believe what she was hearing. Rob killed Black. What the fuck! But she didn't interrupt Tone, she let him get everything off his chest and as much information as she could.

"I know you heard of Black's big brothers that were doing a murder bid from awhile back. But anyway you ain't going to believe this shit. Why the same day they got out was the same day we murdered that nigga. I don't know how they found out who did their peps but obviously they did. So now you know what it is Dee. I'm going to murder their entire family, starting with their mama."

She knew of Black's brothers alright. They were more psychotic than Promise. But she also knew they didn't commit this crime and there shouldn't be any beef brought to their table, especially not their mother's. That was her mother's good friend. She definitely couldn't let anything happen to her.

"Tone, I don't know if I'm hearing wrong or just not understanding. You're telling me that Rob murdered Black because he saw us eating breakfast together? Did he not know my mother and Black's mother were cool? He had to know because they work out together at Fairfax damn near every day. So seeing as though our mothers are friends and we actually grew up together from elementary days, why in the hell would he murder him over fucking breakfast?"

"That's exactly what I tried to tell him. I was there with him when he saw y'all and the shit looked real innocent to me. But he wasn't trying to hear shit I had to say. His main focus was getting Black away from you. So that's what we did."

"Okay wait a minute Tone. You went along with it knowing it was wrong? You helped take an innocent man's life over breakfast?"

"Man Dee, I feel what you're trying to say but that's my brother. Ride or Die."

"I get that. Trust me Tone I do. But it just seems so fucked up. Now my baby has to grow up without a father over some fucking breakfast. Damn!" Divine was saying one thing but thinking another, *please believe my son will not be without his father.*

"That's the same thing I said." He turned around looking out of the back window and saw just about all the family members had gone inside. "It's time for us to go inside Dee. I think they're lining up the family. You can walk beside me."

"Tone, I don't want all that attention right now. You know people pointing and wondering who I am. Like you said no one knew of me and Rob's crazy relationship. Not to mention I hate funerals so I'm just going to stay in the back. But I will come to your mom's house to give her my condolences."

"That's cool Dee, let's go get this shit over with."

Divine did what she said she would. She stood in the back of the funeral looking like the pregnant gangster bitch that she was pretending to give her respects to Rob. She thought he had to be one sick muthafucka to murder a man over breakfast and about a bitch that wasn't even his. She would have never thought in a million years that he was crazy. Yeah he was a street nigga so yeah murder was a part of the game, kill or be killed. To her that didn't make a person crazy. But to take a man's life one should have reason. Not because he had some sick fantasy about her belonging to him and to kill her good friend for it. What she really couldn't believe was that she had spent years fucking this man and these last couple of months getting even closer to him and she didn't sense his dark side.

With Promise she always knew he wasn't wrapped too tight so some of the shit he did didn't even surprise her. Hell, sometimes she even agreed with some of his crazy shit. Now thinking of Promise she was glad Rob didn't know about the two. If he would have brought that shit to her Don's door she would have put the muthafucka down herself.

She walked out of the funeral feeling a little bad for Tone. She was not going to allow him to murder her mother's good friend and family for something they weren't a part of. It was sad to say, but now Tone had to go also. He shouldn't have helped murder her friend over some damn breakfast.

Driving down 71st on her way to her mother's house she thought about what her twin told her years ago. "We might have adopted and perfected this game we're playing but we must never forget about our sister Karma while we're in this shit. Trust when I tell you Doll, she's a bitch. Do her right, she'll do you right but if you do her dirty, she'll do you ten times worse."

Having a crazy moment herself she looked at herself in her rear view mirror with an evil smirk. "It looks like I'm going to have Cedar to myself after all. I guess no one told those niggas about my sister Karma. She ain't just a bitch she's the baddest bitch in the game."

TWENTY THREE

Promise sat up in his king size bed looking around his bedroom at his condo missing Divine. He missed everything about her. He missed simple stuff like waking up to her pretty face. The way her face looked in the morning was the way it looked throughout the day and into the night. He loved the fact that she didn't wear make-up. She was naturally beautiful. He missed staying up late with her talking shit and watching movies. He missed her cooking, walking behind her fat ass and he damn sure missed his heaven, making her cream all in his mouth and on his dick. But what he missed the most for some reason was washing her body. He loved taking his time washing and admiring her body.

Even though he had brought his Queen home and promised to stay by her side he hadn't. He still had unfinished business to take care of.

Dreading to start his day he got out of bed going into the bathroom.

He left the house wearing black Dickie pants, his Timer Warner Cable shirt and jacket, a black skull cap, and black construction steel toe Timbs. He was ready to get down to business.

He pulled in front of an apartment building down on 30th. He sat in his truck for about two hours watching the building activities. He wanted to see who was going in, who was coming out, and how frequent. Once he saw everything he needed he hopped out of his Time Warner Cable van with his tool box in hand. He went inside the building taking two stairs at a time to the second floor. He stood in front of apartment number three then sat his tool box down going to work.

The apartment he stepped into was dark and musty. In the kitchen there were dishes piled in the sink with roaches crawling all over them. The garbage over flowed with roaches crawling out. And right there on the couch was his baby brother Tez with roaches crawling over his ass too.

He couldn't believe what his eyes were seeing in front of him. Dontez Green nodded out with a needle sticking out of his arm. He couldn't fucking believe it. His boy told him he had seen his brother looking sick, but damn. Tez had to be the most spoiled nigga on the planet. He had any and every thing a teenage boy could want and even more. And he didn't have to get his hands dirty to get it. Promise had made sure he didn't want for anything and all his siblings for that matter. He did all the dirty work and took all the risk. But he guessed that was the kind of shit muthafuckas didn't appreciate if they weren't getting the shit themselves.

Now his baby brother was laid out on the couch doped the fuck out and off heroin at that. What were the fucking odds? His brother was addicted to the very thing he had been pushing in the streets for the past six years.

He walked over to his brother tapping his leg several times.

Tez barely lifted his eyes and smiled, "Ain't this some shit. Kinsman County's King down here with the common folk. What's up big bro?"

"Nigga you! Why you down here pushing that shit in yo' arm and our mother is laid up in the hospital fighting for her life?"

He started to nod out again but Promise kicked him trying to make him stay awake.

"Fuck Innocence. Why the fuck I care if she's fighting for her life? She don't give a fuck about me. If it ain't about yo punk ass then it ain't about shit."

"Well since I see you're feeling a certain way about my momma, just tell me why. I know it was you. Why did you do her like that?"

"Because I wanted to, she ain't shit but a lying bitch. Both y'all muthafuckas are the reason why my daddy ain't around and smoking that crack shit. Hell if I was him, I would have left too. She treated you better than all her other kids and even her husband. I bet she'll think twice about that favoritism shit now. She has five kids, not fucking one. I guess she figured no one was going to find out. But anybody could figure that shit out if they took a closer look. The only thing I don't understand is my daddy is the one that stayed with her ass even married her, not yours. So why the fuck did you get all the special treatment? Like I said fuck her, I hope her ass dies."

Shaking his head Promise stood over his brother. "I see you really was feeling a certain way. You real long winded with that shit running through you."

"Nigga, that's because you blowing my shit. And I ain't got shit else to get right with. Punk muthafucka, so say what you came to say so I can go cop me something."

"Well Brother I really ain't got shit to say. All I really want to know is, did yo' daddy have something to do with that shit you did to my mother? I mean you're my brother so you I can't do shit about you but like you said, yo' daddy ain't shit to me."

"Nigga my daddy ain't got shit to do with it. if that was the case he wouldn't have stayed with her lying ass all those years. All he did was finally told me the truth. So nigga fuck you and yo' momma. Now could you leave out of here? I got to cop me some shit."

Promise thought *this is too damn easy.* "Yeah nigga I'm going to leave. But I'm going to say this to you one time and one time only, STAY THE FUCK OFF KINSMAN. Because if you don't I won't give a shit about you being my brother. And if yo' bitch ass got some money I got the shit you need. This shit down here probably down played anyway."

Tez was happier than a muthafucka. Kinsman had the best dog food out there. Hell yeah the shit down there was weak but it also got the job done. "You ain't got to worry about me coming up there. So why don't you let me get some of that as a going away present?"

Promise smiled knowing his dumb ass would fall for it. He threw a couple packs on the table telling his brother to have a nice life. He then walked out knowing the next time he saw his brother it would be in a casket.

The very moment Promise walked out of the door Tez got down to business. He shot that shit in his veins so fast his head was spinning. He slowly started nodding enjoying the feel of that good Kinsman County shit. His head nodded down to his chest with drool sliding out of the corners of his mouth. Too bad that was going to be the last heroin high he was going to ever experience.

TWENTY FOUR

Promise of course didn't keep his promises again. Saying he wasn't going to leave her side, please. He got her home sat under her for about three days and was back in the streets. Talking about he had something very important to take care of, yeah right. But she wasn't about to bitch to him. Her pregnancy was almost over. Then she would be back to her normal self and he would be trailing behind her again with his tongue hanging out of his mouth trying to get a lick.

Now she and Cherokee sat inside the Cheesecake Factory at Legacy Village enjoying an early dinner after finishing up the last of their Christmas shopping. Ever since Sincere had introduced the two they quickly became good friends. This was odd for Divine because she did not do females too often. Yeah she had Promise's sisters but they weren't close at all. She guessed it was a jealousy thing. Her only female friends were her mother and Innocence. So these past three weeks that she has been back home her and Cherokee had become very close. If Sincere would have introduced them sooner she wouldn't have been hanging around with Rob's crazy ass.

Cherokee had been a big help to her with getting the rest of the house together and the rest of the things she needed for the baby. They really just sat in the house and ordered the majority of things on-line. When the furniture was delivered they just pointed to where she wanted the items to go. They even did the majority of their Christmas shopping on-line also. She just wanted to stay stress free and not worry about the house and Promise's ass again.

Savoring the taste Divine took another bite of her salmon. She loved the salmon at the Cheesecake Factory. She couldn't figure out how they kept it so moist. "Kee, I'm telling you I'm going back there in that kitchen and kidnap the chef when we get ready to leave."

"Girl you're crazy as hell and I don't know where you're going to keep him if you do. I don't know Promise too well but I can kind of get a sense that he doesn't play about you."

"Please, that nigga be faking like fuck. Promise might love me to death but for some reason he can't sit around me longer than three minutes."

Taking a sip of her lemon water and wiping her mouth, "If you say so Vine, but the little time I have seen you two together I'm telling you he doesn't take his eyes off of you. Especially your ass I swear it looks like he is drooling at the mouth."

"Well thanks for that bit of information because I thought with me being big as hell he wasn't interested anymore. Not to mention my pussy. Girl do you know I had to go to the spa to get my pussy waxed. When Promise and I started fucking he has always been the one to keep my shit together. So when we were going through our little thing I didn't bother to shave. When I did want to I couldn't even get to it like I really needed to. I was scared I was going to cut my damn self. So when we got shit back on track I just knew that was going to be the first thing he did. But he ain't even looked at me twice. And you know this baby is due in a week and I can't go into the delivery room with a damn jungle between my legs. Kee, that wax shit hurt so bad I cursed his ass out every time she pulled a strip."

Cherokee was falling out of her chair laughing, "Vine your ass is crazy. Why didn't you just tell him to shave you?"

"It's like this Kee Baby, he might have not looked at me twice but at the same time he has. I know Promise, my first day home he saw that my pussy hair was out of control. So now that I got it waxed earlier today believe me when I tell you he's going to have a problem with it. He had to have figured out I couldn't do it myself or it would have been done. You see what I'm getting at?"

"Yeah I see, he's going to hit the roof wondering who you let near your shit."

"Exactly but enough about me and my shit, how are you and my triplet doing?"

Cherokee stated laughing again, "I thought y'all were twins. Where did the triplets come from?"

"Girl because of that little Shereè of yours, I don't care what you say your daughter looks like Sincere. Are you sure you two never fucked before?"

"Trust me if we had I would remember that shit. That big ass dick Sincere got I don't believe there's a female he fucked on this earth that can forget his ass."

"TMI, Cherokee, TMI"

"I'm sorry girl just thinking about him makes me want to, oh sorry again TMI right."

"Yeah, but on that note I think it's time for us to get up out of here. I want to stop by the hospital before I go home."

Cherokee paid for their food and then they left and went their separate ways.

After spending the rest of evening with Innocence, Divine couldn't wait to get into bed. But she really didn't want to leave the hospital because she could have sworn she felt Innocence's fingers twitch when she was holding her hand. It happened every time she mentioned Promise's name. Then she thought she was just tired and her mind was playing tricks on her. She told Innocence she would be back tomorrow. She wanted to see if the same thing would happen again.

※※※※※※

Divine sat up in the bed thinking about Promise and how the avoidance shit stops today. Every time they had an issue with one another that's what they did, avoid each other. And that shit was getting old.

When Promise walked through the bedroom door he was surprised to see his Baby Doll still awake. He had been trying to stay out until he knew she was asleep. He walked over to the bed and gave her a kiss on the forehead.

"What you still doing up, Doll?"

She gave him a look that let him know she had an attitude, "I'm waiting to talk to you."

"Now or when I get out of the shower?"

She pushed the cover off, hopped out of bed and started to the bathroom. "We can talk while you're in the shower."

He wanted to kick himself. He didn't want to be in the bathroom alone with her. And she got on that damn short ass night shirt with half her ass hanging out. He should have just sat his ass down on the side of the bed.

When he walked into the bathroom she was sitting on the bench looking like she was ready to kill something. Trying not to give her too much eye contact he undressed and stepped into the shower. While he was washing up he waited to hear what she had to say but it never happened. He turned off the water and pulled back the shower glass only to see she wasn't there anymore. He dried off and slid on some basketball shorts.

She looked at him coming out of the bathroom with his shorts on and knew now for sure he was full of shit.

"Don, I'm going to say this one time and one time only. This shit we got is over. You don't want me, but it would kill you if someone else had me. That's the only reason you pulled that captain save a hoe move. But you ain't got to worry about that shit again. I won't be the one disappearing this time. Tomorrow I want you and your shit out of here. You can move back into the condo which won't be hard for you anyway seeing as though that's where you are until you decide to feel sorry for me and come home. But you ain't got to bless me with your presence no more. You coming here is pointless. So do us both a favor and stop pretending and stay the fuck away." With that being said she rolled over and let the tears fall from her eyes.

He walked over and got into bed behind her. He pulled her shoulder so she could turn to him.

She didn't budge, she just spoke, "Don't even try it. There is nothing else to be said. I hope whatever or whoever you're doing is making you happy. But know you better enjoy it while you can because once I have this baby, I'm going to bring hell to your front door steps."

He smiled. He loved when she threatened him. That shit turned him on big time. He has always loved when she was in Boss Bitch mode. But he'd never let her know that shit.

So this time he climbed over her and lay directly in her face, but he wasn't wearing a smile anymore. "I ain't going anywhere and before you even fix yo mouth to say it, neither are you. Now you wanted to talk so talk."

"Don, I can't stand your ass. Why can't you be real with yourself and with me for once? You don't want me so why won't you let me go? Really you talk that shit you're not going to leave my side. Then I don't see you anymore. I just feel when you come lay in bed in the middle of the night. You were so worried about that nigga fucking yo pussy and nuttin'…"

Before she could even finish her sentence he was face to face, nose to nose, and lips to lips with her. He spoke slowly through clenched teeth, "I'm begging you not to go there Divine Nanette. Do not fucking do it. Say what the fuck you got to say without all this extra dramatic bullshit. Do you understand me?"

She couldn't take it anymore so she gave up. It was no use to talking to him. Once she had her baby she could show him better than she could tell him.

She moved away from him turning on her other side not even caring anymore. "I don't have anything to say but good night Promise."

"When the fuck did I become Promise?"

"You have always been Promise."

"Not when you're speaking directly to me, never. So where does this Promise shit come from all of a sudden?" He asked as he moved close to her and put his arm around her.

She had a thousand tears coming down her face. She was starting to think he liked seeing her miserable. He got off on the shit. Sick muthafucka. "I didn't even realize that, you just told me something new."

"What the fuck eva Doll, you know what you're doing. All I'm asking is once you have my son please don't try me. Just in case that's what you're thinking, please don't."

He rolled on his back and looked up at the ceiling with his hands behind his head. He knew what was wrong with him. He knew why he wasn't coming home. But how does he tell her that? She's supposed to know him better than he knows himself. She should already know what his problem is. Why can't she just ride this one out? Shit he's got to. Before he never had to tell her what was wrong, she would tell him. He'd be glad his damn self when this pregnant shit was over with. This emotional shit just wasn't for him.

He took a deep breath, "I know what I told you and I apologize for my behavior, me not being around and what not. But Baby Doll, do you know how hard it is for me to be around you? Doll it drives me crazy being around your big juicy sexy pregnant ass and not being able to touch. I know the doctor said it was cool, but baby I don't want to take any chances. Every time I'm home and you walk that fat ass past me my mind starts going crazy. So to contain myself, I just try and stay away. But I promise you once the baby is born and your body heals, I'm going to fuck the shit out of you. And for the record the last thing you should be concerned about is me not wanting you and me laying pipe somewhere else. When I go to the condo I lie in that bed, close my eyes, and jack-off to that fat ass you got. Please believe me."

She had a gut feeling of why he wasn't coming home but she wasn't sure. Her feeling was confirmed when Cherokee told her he looked as if he were drooling at the mouth when he looked at her ass. So why did she have to hear him say it. It really didn't matter because it was said and she knew how to put an end to all this madness.

She pulled the cover back, got on her knees, and looked toward the bathroom door so that her back was directly to him. She pulled her night shirt over her head and threw it to the floor. She bent over so she was on all fours. She made sure he couldn't see anything but her freshly waxed pussy and her wide ass that was all for him. She looked back over her left shoulder pleading with him, "Daddy please, she missed you so much. She needs you, please come back home."

Promise lay still in his same position. He didn't move. His breaths quickened as his chest rose and fell. "Who the fuck touched mines, Divine Nanette?"

She smiled on the inside. She knew he would notice. "I went to the spa. She was way out of control."

He looked at her cleaned waxed pussy from the back. He knew it was a professional job, but who the fuck gave her permission to let someone near the gates of his heaven. He pulled his shorts off and mounted himself behind her.

When she saw his thick beautiful dick jump out of his shorts her pussy started throbbing and juices started racing down her legs. *What the fuck has he done to my body to make it respond to him on sight like that?* She was damn near shaking anticipating his dicks arrival. Now thinking, *I let someone touch his heaven, I'm in big trouble and I'm about to get my brains fucked out.*

He rubbed his hands all over her juicy ass. He held her hips moving her back and forth slowly without entering her. "Did I give you permission to let someone near my shit Baby Doll?" Whoop! He smacked her ass then rubbed it in the exact same spot.

She wasn't prepared for what he had just done or for what he had done after. She tried to pull away but he wasn't having it.

"Don't even try it!" He pulled her back. Whoop! He smacked and rubbed her ass again.

She screamed a sexy scream. She couldn't believe it. Wasn't shit sexy about what he was doing to her or was it? "Please Don, no more."

Whoop! He smacked and rubbed her ass again. "That's not answering my question. I asked did I give you motherfucking permission." Whoop! He smacked and rubbed again.

She panted and screamed even sexier than before. "No Don, you didn't and I promise it won't ever happen again."

"It better not." Whoop! He smacked her ass but this time he didn't rub. He buried his juicy dick deep inside his heaven.

Instantly from the moment the head of his dick touched her pussy hole she started cumming "Oh shit Don…wait a minute…. Baby please wait… what the fuck…I'm cummin'…oh my God…what the fuck…"

Her pussy muscles pulsated and gripped his dick but he wasn't falling for that shit this time. She had been a very bad girl.

She wasn't prepared for what he was doing to her body. She couldn't believe it. Usually she only came when he ate her pussy, sucked her right breast something else she didn't understand, and when she felt his seed cuming inside of her. His nut was like a trigger for her, she got off knowing she had control over his dick. She never let anyone or anything have control over her. But now what the hell was he doing to her? Her body was responding without her approval.

He kept smacking, rubbing, and digging even deeper inside her and "Oh…. what the fuck…." flew out of her mouth as she had another orgasm. "Don, please...hold up baby…just for sec…please…"

He didn't let up. He put a pillow under her stomach for her to lie on. He put her legs together tight and his legs on the outside of hers then lifted her butt just a little. He smacked, rubbed and dug some more in her pussy. On the fourth deep stroke she couldn't believe it. She grabbed the sheets with her head down and screamed in the mattress as her body came again, panting, "Please no more…. I can't take it anymore…."

He took his left knee and pushed up her left leg, digging in just a little deeper and grinding just a little faster he gasped, "Yes the fuck you can and yes the fuck you will. Didn't you realize your God was missing his heaven? Didn't you know what was going to happen when you bent this fat ass over and begged for me to come back home? Now that you got me where you wanted me to be Baby Doll, I want to feel you cum on my dick one more time. Promise me you're going to cum for daddy." Stroking her pussy even deeper, "I'm not playing with you anymore. Now give your God what the fuck he wants." Whoop! He smacked, rubbed, and dug even more.

She panted "Don....please stop...I can't...cum no more."

Whoop! "I said cum now," he demanded.

She couldn't believe it, what he was doing to her body was sinful.

"Oh....my....fuckin'....God....Dontae....yes....yes ....yes....yes....Baby your heaven cumming...yes" And this time when he felt her pussy muscles pulsate Promise came along with her, screaming "Baby Doll....."

TWENTY FIVE

Promise lay in bed not able to sleep. He was focused on Divine. She was moaning while tossing and turning in her sleep. He watched her wondering what she was dreaming of. But when she moaned like she was in agonizing pain he knew it was time to wake her.

He gave her shoulder a soft nudge, "Baby Doll, Baby wake up."

She didn't budge.

"Baby Doll, I need you to wake up Baby."

She slowly opened her eyes. Once she was fully alert she felt as if something was turning her stomach inside out. She immediately groaned, grabbed her stomach and curled up in the fetal position.

Promise was now terrified seeing his Baby Doll like this. He rushed to her aid. "Doll, are you okay? Tell me what's wrong."

Looking up at him with tears in her eyes she tried to tell him what she was feeling. "Don, my stomach and back hurt so bad. I don't know Baby, but I feel like I need to use the bathroom real bad."

He helped her out of bed and into the bathroom. She was holding her stomach the entire way telling him how much her stomach was cramping.

In the bathroom he sat her on the toilet. He stood over her in silence watching her. He had been at a loss of words since he saw the tears in her eyes.

After she used the toilet he got the tissue and wiped his heaven. He looked at the tissue and his eyes got as big as saucers at what he saw. There was a lot of creamy looking stuff with blood in it. Now his heart was beating fast.

"Damn Doll, I knew we shouldn't have did shit." He held the tissue to where she could see. "Look you're bleeding again."

She looked at the tissue then at his worried eyes. "Don, I think that's my mucus plug. The doctor told me I should be expecting to see it sometime this week." At that moment she got another sharp pain in her back crawling around to her stomach. She sighed and took a deep breath.

He stared at her going through the motions. He dropped the tissue in the toilet then flushed it with her still sitting there. He then washed and dried his hands. He grabbed her hand and led her back to the bedroom sitting her down on her lounge reading chair. Not saying a word to her he proceeded to their walk-in closet. When he came out he was fully dressed in a polo jogging suit with his wheat construction Timbs on his feet and he had everything he needed to dress her. He put her on some granny Hanes Her Way panties, a bra, and a Juicy Couture jogging suit. He slid her Uggs boots on her feet and her Guess pea-coat around her shoulders. He grabbed her bag that she had already packed for the hospital weeks ago and her hand.

"Come on. We're going to the hospital. And if anything has happened to my son because your ass was dying for some dick I'm going to hurt you Baby Doll."

With that they were out the door in his black on black Dodge Charger and on their way to St. Luke hospital.

⊗⊗⊗⊗⊗⊗

Innocence could feel herself slipping away. She saw her best friend Simone reaching out to her saying it was time for her to come home. She could hear Simone telling her all her pains would go away if she just took her hand.

She told her friend, "I can't come yet, it's not time. Our children still need me."

Her best friend moved closer to her and stroked the side of her face. "They don't need you anymore, they're grown now. You have suffered enough. You deserve not to hurt anymore."

She looked at her best friend and saw nothing but peacefulness on her face. She wanted that. She was tired of the lies, secrets, and worries. One of her secrets had caused her to be beaten nearly to death by her own son because of jealousy.

She stroked her friends face also. "I know they're grown but they still need me. I can't leave them with so many unanswered questions. I can't leave that burden on their hearts, especially my boy Promise. Simone, I wish you would have had more time with Sincere. He has grown to become such a handsome young man. Every

Sunday we spend time together cooking, eating, and me telling him about the good ole days. I know he's losing his mind because I've been gone so long. And if you would have met Divine, you would love her as if she was your own. She comes and talks to me every day with a heavy heart. She told me that she really needs me right now. She's having a baby and Promise is giving her hell. So I'm sorry I can't join you yet. I have a family I have to get back in order and I can feel my grandbaby. He's on his way very soon."

Simone gave her a kiss on the cheek, "Innocence, I understand. Please tell Sincere that I love him and I'm so sorry I left him so soon. Please keep taking good care of my boy. I love you best friend."

"And I love you too, Simone." Innocence turned her back and walked away from the only friend she has ever truly had. She turned back around and waved bye for the second time in their lives.

※※※※※

Promise held Divine's hand coaching her the best way he could. He hated seeing her in pain but yet at the same moment she looked so beautiful to him. But one thing was for sure and two was for certain his beautiful Queen wasn't cooperating with the doctors at all. He rubbed her head, kissed her dry lips, and whispered in her ear, "Baby Doll, you're the strongest female I have ever met and this is something I know you can handle. Baby I'm ready to meet my son. I'm ready to spoil the young

God. So please for me can you give them one more good push?"

She shook her head yes and he kissed her dry lips again telling her thank you.

He moved back to his original position where he could see everything. From where he stood he could actually see the hair on his son's head. He pushed her right leg back and told the doctor to just say when.

Dr. Frazier looked at the monitor and could tell another contraction was on the way. She placed two fingers at the bottom of Divine's vagina looking at Promise saying, "When".

He looked up and locked eyes with his heart. "Baby Doll, I need a nice big push. It's time for our legacy to be born.

Never taking her eyes from his, she nodded her head up and down.

She gave it everything she had. She pushed and pushed with him cheering her on. "That's it baby, don't stop. Come on Doll, real hard baby." She pushed real hard one last time then she felt her son's head push out of her vagina.

He looked at her and smiled, "good Baby, but the doc said one more time. We have to get his body out."

She pushed again and felt her son slither all the way out of her.

The doctor gave Promise the scissors to cut the umbilical cord.

Drowsily Divine said, "Don I don't hear him, why don't I hear him?"

And as soon as she finished asking the question she heard her son's beautiful cry.

Doctor Frazier handed Promise his son never mentioning through this whole ordeal about the guy who was coming to the appointments with Divine.

He held his son in his arms admiring him for the first time. He kissed him on the forehead with body fluid on him and all. "December 24, my young God has arrived, Merry Christmas to me."

"Baby let me see him."

He looked over at Divine like he had forgotten she was even in the room. He walked over to her and gave her his son.

She looked at her baby in awe. He was so beautiful. His skin color was nothing like hers. He was as yellow as Promise even though that's not where he inherited it from. Her mother was just as light. His hair was jet black slicked around his head like he had a wrap. He had light brown eyes like Promise's also, but they weren't from him either. Her grandmother had the same eyes. His nose belonged all to her and he had the most beautiful set of juicy lips. Looking at them made her think of his biological father because they definitely belonged to him. But at first glance anyone could mistake him for Promise's son. Well why wouldn't they, that's exactly who he was.

She stroked her son's cheek, "Promise he's so beautiful. But Baby I haven't even picked out a name for him, what are we going to name him?"

He leaned over and gave her forehead a kiss, then his son's. "I named him the very day Sincere told me we were having a boy." He reached and took the baby from her. He looked at his son's perfect face, "His name is Knowledge Marquise Green."

She smiled repeating her son's name, "Knowledge Marquise Green."

The nurses took Knowledge from his Dad so they could clean him up.

There was a slight tap at the door. Sincere poked his head inside, "has the young Don arrived?"

"Yes he has," Promise replied smiling from ear to ear.

"Good because Innocence is awake and she says she wants her Promise.

TWENTY
SIX

Promise lay on his mother's couch with his son on his chest while he watched television. He was so ready to go home, take a shower and climb into bed. His son was only four weeks old and his Queen couldn't keep her ass out of the streets. Talking about she had to put things back in order. Wasn't shit out of order she just wanted an excuse to get her ass out of the house. But he didn't mind her getting out. He felt she deserved a little fresh air. And he used the time she was gone to spend with his mother and his son.

He was so happy to have his life back. He went to her house and chilled every chance he got. Innocence came out of her coma like nothing had ever happened to her. He told her what he had to do to his brother and how it hurt him to put him down. But he wasn't downright heartless towards his flesh and blood. After the demise of Tez, he did give him a proper burial with only close family. Innocence didn't shed a tear for her youngest son because what he did to her was unforgivable. He had too much jealousy and larceny in his heart to move on in his life. Then with him being addicted to heroin didn't make the situation any better. Him living would have only been miserable for himself, so she felt he was in a better place.

Promise glanced over at his mother and knew it was time for him to learn the truth about his life. He was tired of putting puzzle pieces together. She had always been real and honest about any and everything except for how he came about. He hoped she didn't think he was stupid. He knew that he and his siblings didn't share the same father.

"Ma, can we talk?"

"Of course we can son, what do you want to talk about?"

"Ma, I'm tired of you talking in riddles about me. Saying little shit here and there. Tez let it be known why your husband left. That's where a lot of his pain originated from. His dad told him I was the reason he couldn't stay with his family and that I was the reason he was smoking that shit. I mean Ma, I'm a grown man now with my own son. I think it is time for me to know the truth."

She took a deep breath. She knew he was right. He had a right to know why her so called husband and her youngest son hated him so much.

"Well son, I don't know where to begin."

"Why not the beginning, Ma I promise I can handle it."

"I know you can baby. I just don't want you questioning your existence when it's all over. But I'm going to give you the truth because you do deserve to know."

Taking another deep breath, "Your father, well the man I wanted you to believe was your father tried to live that street life shit. He had started doing business with a big time drug dealer but he really didn't know what he was getting himself into or me for that matter. I really didn't know what he was doing. My ass was young and naïve. One day when I came home from work from my little STNA job he gave me a bag telling me it was flour and he needed me to take it back to this guy because it wasn't any good. I really wasn't thinking being naïve and all. I went to the guy's house and rang the doorbell. When he came to the door I held up the flour telling him what Big Dee said. He snatched the door open and pulled me inside. I stood in his front door way for about five minutes holding the flour with him staring at me. I didn't know what to feel or think because the look he was giving me was scaring me half to death. He finally broke the silence asking me why Dee didn't bring it himself. Why would he send me? I told him I didn't know. I just did what he asked me to do. He took the flour from me and told me to sit on the couch while he went into the kitchen. When he came back he told me how Dee must not love me or care shit about my wellbeing. He asked me my name. I told him and he said my name fitted me perfectly. He said lil Ms. Innocence, innocent and green to the game. I didn't have a clue what the hell he was talking about."

She looked over at Promise wondering if she should go on. As she looked at him she saw his real father's eyes staring back at her and knew she had to. He deserved this.

"Well to make a long story short son, you know it wasn't flour. It was heroin and Dee stole out of the package he was supposed to sell. And he sent my young dumb ass to the guy's house to return the goods, talking about the dope wasn't right. Now the guy was a heartless, ruthless dope man. So I ended up locked in a room being raped repeatedly for weeks waiting for Dee to come up with the guy's money."

Promise sat up on the couch with his son in his arms trying not to believe what he just heard. His mother had been raped. And at that moment it didn't take a rocket scientist to figure out the ending. He was the product of that rape. His heart rate had increased. He didn't know what to fucking feel at that moment. He didn't know if he should hate her husband or the man who raped her. They both did her dirty. And at that moment in his mind they both had to die.

She had stopped talking because she saw the wheels turning in his head. She didn't know if she should go on.

He stared at his mother, his life, his world. How could someone hurt something as beautiful as her? Yeah a lot of people thought she was mean and hateful but she was never that way with him. Then he thought about his heart, Divine. It's always the good ones that are done dirty turning them into heartless women. He had to know more.

"Don't stop Ma, please tell me everything."

Leaning her head back and closing her eyes she continued. "Well, the son of a bitch never showed. He never came for me. The guy was right about him not caring about me. But during the time I was there I guess the guy took a liking to me. He didn't let me leave his house and if I did I was always with him. He hated that I was put in that situation so that's when I got schooled to the game. He wanted to make sure no one ever did me wrong again. I can remember one day we were out riding doing his rounds and I saw someone from my past standing inside of a phone booth. When I saw him I guess I looked like I saw a ghost which made him ask me who the man was. I told him no one and he stared at me asking me never to lie to him. So I told him the truth. I told him the man was my uncle and he used to molest me when I was five years old."

Promise could have sworn his heart stopped when she said that. His mother was molested, what the hell. He gave himself a mental note to ask about her uncle when she finished talking because he definitely was going to murder that nigga. She was only five fucking years old.

"I know what you're thinking son and there's no need. After I told him about the man he turned his car around, parked, got out of the car, pulled out his gun and blew my uncle's brains out. I couldn't believe it. He shot him in broad daylight in my face. He killed him for molesting me and yet he had kept me and raped me so far for two months. Now I had to be the one that was crazy because for some odd reason I felt grateful to him. He had killed the man who had been haunting my dreams. Anyway another month had passed and I had missed my period. He told me with the life he lived he couldn't raise a child but he also didn't want me to kill his baby. Somehow he caught up with Dee. Come to find out he had skipped town. He told him it was safe to come home and he wasn't going to kill him but it had a catch to it. He told him he had to marry and stay with me. Of course Dee bitch ass agreed and so did I because I didn't want to bring a child into the world without a husband. I went back home never telling Dee I was pregnant. But he wasn't a stupid man. He knew the child I was carrying wasn't his but he was also too afraid of the guy to say anything. Yet he never questioned me about the three months that I was missing from home. I guess he thought I was dead and was surprised when he got the message from the guy. When I made it back to my apartment I got a visit from a man that used to stop by the guy's house when I was there. He gave me some keys, told me an address, and that my child would always be taken care of. At this moment right now we're sitting in the house that the keys and address had belonged to. And every month after I moved in I have been receiving a money order in the mail for a thousand dollars. Once I had more children the money order went up to four thousand every month still to this day."

"Wait Ma, you're telling me that a man raped you, got you pregnant, sent you back to your man, bought you a house and is still taking care of you?"

"I know it seems too farfetched to be real, but it's the truth son. But anyway a while back Big Dee found out about the money and finally put two and two together about the house while rambling through my mail. He felt I was betraying him. He said it was bad enough that he accepted the guy's son because he always felt you weren't his but for me to still have some relationship with the guy was unacceptable. So he left not even caring that I did have four that were rightfully his. But before he left I told him he had never accepted my son and he can go on about his business anyway. I was tired of living a lie, because I had lost all love for him when he left me for dead. But Promise I didn't want you to be without a father which was the reason why I went along with the bullshit in the first place. Then after I got pregnant with your sister I definitely wasn't trying to be alone. I also told Big Dee that your real father took better care of all my children more than he ever had. Son, and to make this even crazier I never knew your father's true identity. And I know you Promise. I can see murder in your eyes. Just like him someone hurt me so that's what you want to do. Kill the man who raped me. But son, in some fucked up crazy way I got a lot of love for the man. He didn't know me from a can of paint. He could have killed me but instead he schooled me to this fucked up game out here, killed for me, and still to this day takes care of me and my children."

Promise couldn't digest everything she had told him. In his head he kept saying *I'm a fucking rape baby, a fucking rape baby* "A muthafuckin' rape baby," slipped out of his mouth.

His mother got out of her chair, walked over to her son and sat down beside him. "You're no such thing. What you are is meant to be. Don't you know by now Promise that you were destined for greatness? Just like my grandbaby Knowledge here." She took Knowledge out of Promise's arms and held him to her chest placing soft kisses on his forehead.

"I heard every word Baby Doll spoke to me when I was in that coma. I know he's not your biological son but just like you he was meant to be. And I'll be damned if anybody says anything different. Even Divine herself. Son

I don't want you to go around with all that negative stuff on your heart about being a rape baby. Because in my heart I honestly believe that even though I was held in that house against my will by the second month it wasn't rape anymore. Trust me when I tell you you were conceived out of some twisted fucked up, psychotic love shit. But it was love, there's no denying that. And just like your name, I promised to always love you with all my heart."

She gave her oldest and favorite son a kiss on the cheek. "Now I got my grandbaby. It's time for you to get out of here and go find your wife. I don't want her running in them streets by herself because the next baby will for sure be yours."

"Ma, I ain't worried about that. Baby Doll ain't going anywhere. Even if she wanted to her heart, mind, body, and soul wouldn't allow it. That's all me. Knowledge was conceived before she became mine but he is without a doubt my son. But I will take you up on the baby sitting offer because you put a lot of shit on my brain. So I need to go clear my head and relax and only my Baby Doll can handle that.

He gave his mother and son a kiss and left to get served by his Queen.

✖✖✖✖✖✖

Divine thought it was time to pay her little brother Jay a visit. Cedar had been without a supplier long enough. Now it was time for her to flood Cedar streets with Kinsman County's dope.

She had confided in Sincere about what Rob and Tone did to Black the day of Rob's funeral. So they took care of Tone a week after his brother's home going. They did the job together not involving anyone from the Fam. Not even Promise.

She didn't even want to tell Promise how crazy Rob had turned out to be about her. In his twisted head he would have wanted to know what the fuck she had done to him to make him have those feelings for her. In reality she hadn't done anything special for Rob to act the way he did. Shit she didn't do anything special to Promise in the beginning for his ass to be as crazy as he was. But she couldn't say that now.

Since she had their son and couldn't have sex she had been giving him head morning, noon, and night. Without him even telling her he needed to relax. She loved sucking his dick. And she took advantage every chance she got because she knew once the doctor gave him the okay she wasn't going to get the opportunity to feel him in her mouth for weeks. She knew his head and his dick were going to be buried in her pussy. She probably wouldn't even make it out of the bedroom for weeks.

That's the reason she had been trying to take care of everything getting Cedar ready before her six weeks were up.

TWENTY SEVEN

Sincere was awakened at 9:00 o'clock in the morning with the feeling of Cherokee sliding down his dick. He loved the fact she was a freak and couldn't get enough of his dick. He opened his eyes slowly and saw his angel staring down at him with ecstasy written all over her face as always. He took his big hands and gripped both of her small ass cheeks, spreading them apart guiding her up and down his dick.

She squeezed her own breast, "Oh Sincere...Baby you're making my pussy feel so good...I don't think you know how much I love this dick...."

He smacked her on the ass, "That's...the only thing you love about me is my dick...." He pulled her up to the tip of his dick and rammed it inside of her over and over again.

"No Baby I also love you but, Yeah baby right there...Damn Sin....When you got all this dick inside me....I can't think about anything else....Oh yeah Sin right there baby....please don't stop...."

Hearing her say that made him really start grinding himself in and out of her pussy. He heard her say she loved him. He has been waiting to hear those words from her for weeks. He knew for sure he loved her. But it was sad to say because he would never speak the same three words he had been yearning to hear.

He gripped her ass even tighter and guided her up real slowly to the tip of his dick and back down even slower. He kept with the same motion loving how her pussy felt gripping his dick.

She thought she was going to go insane. "Oh my God Sin please don't stop. Baby please. God-damn right there, I'm cumming...."

She couldn't take the motions he was putting her though. She started squeezing her breast even tighter, "Oh my God....I'm cumming again....Shit...." And this time when she released Sincere came along with her, "Damn Kee....Fuck...."

She collapsed on his chest trying to catch her breath with him hugging her tight. He lifted her head gently and kissed her juicy lips. She laid her head back on his chest then drifted off to sleep.

As she slept Sincere thought how important she has become to his life. He could remember going days without seeing or talking to her and now he couldn't even go hours. He had to have her in his apartment waiting on him every night when he got home. His closet was full of her clothes and his second bedroom was full of her daughter's things. At that moment he knew it was time for him to face the facts. He was in love with her and wanted her and her daughter there with him permanently. He knew it meant taking a chance bringing her all the way in his life style but it was a chance he was willing to take.

He stroked her back, "Come on Kee, it's time to get up. We need to get ready to pick up my baby girl. Did you hear me Bay?"

"Yes Sin, just give me five more minutes please."

Smacking her on her ass, "Nope, you shouldn't have been trying to be a big girl jumping on my shit early in the AM. Now come on, I promised my baby girl I would take her shoe shopping. Some little girl in her class got some light up shoes and she wants some. And you know anything my baby girl wants, she gets."

She climbed off of him and stepped out of bed, "Sincere, you can't keep spoiling her like that. I won't be able to keep up with the life style you're introducing her to. It's bad enough Divine won't keep her out of the mall."

He sat up on the side of the bed with his face turned up, "Why would you have to keep up?"

"I mean Sin, when this is over. I don't want her thinking I can give her anything she wants like you do."

"Cherokee, gone somewhere with that shit, you ain't going nowhere. And even if so I will always take care of my baby girl. But if your ass does try to stray you better believe I won't do a damn thing for your ass, just Sheree'." He walked past her slapping her on the ass as he went into the bathroom to jump in the shower.

※※※※※※

Divine's six week appointment was at 9:30 in the morning but Promise had her there at 9 o'clock. He wasn't taking any chances of being late. He even dropped their son off to his mother the night before. No chances.

Her doctor gave her the exam and gave her a clean bill of health. She told Promise he has the green light now that Divine had healed perfectly.

After leaving Kaiser at the Severance Center Promise drove straight down Euclid Hts. Ave to his destination. He pulled in front of the Inner Continental Hotel for the valet service. He held Divine's hand while leading her into the hotel and to their room.

"Really Promise, at 10:30 in the morning. We just couldn't have gone back home?"

He stopped in front of the Presidential Suite and looked at her, "Don't you ever in yo life question anything I do. Especially when it's dealing with mines. Do you understand me?" He spoke sternly staring directly into her eyes.

She nodded her head up and down slowly. He had just turned her on. She didn't realize how much she had missed his aggressiveness. He had been so loving and gentle since their son had been born.

Gazing into his eyes she wrapped her arms around him and spoke softly, "Damn, I've missed you so much Daddy. I apologize. I will never question you again."

He squeezed her ass, "I know you won't. But now I got to punish that ass." He opened their door and led her inside.

She stood at the door in awe. The room looked magnificent. He had out done himself as usual. He had everything set up beautifully. The curtains were closed making the room appear dark even though it was early in the morning. There were candles burning with rose pedals spread across the bed and throughout the suite. There was a platter of fresh fruit and wine chilling beside the Jacuzzi as soft music played in the background. The Jacuzzi sat in the middle of the floor full of bubbles inviting her in.

He led her to the bathroom and slowly undressed her and himself placing their clothes on the lounge bench. He then led her to the Jacuzzi holding her hand so she could ease down inside. He sat behind her and gave her a glass of wine. He fed her some strawberries and kissed her small juicy lips. She tried telling him how happy she was but he stopped her. After her glass of wine he washed every nook and cranny of her body. When he got to his heaven he simply admired the craftsmanship of her neatly shaven pussy that he had given her last night. He placed soft kisses on the face of his heaven. When he finished cleaning and drying them both he led her to the bed. He laid her on her stomach and proceeded to massage her entire back side with warming oil from the tip of her neck down to the tip of her toes.

She felt as if she was in Heaven. This was one of those times she knew she would be in tears. She loved Promise's aggressiveness but she also loved when he took his time with her treating her like a Goddess.

He went back to massaging her ass giving it his undivided attention. She felt his soft lips kissing and biting her ass cheeks. Her body starting tingling all over and that's when she felt the first tear escape from her eye sliding down to the pillow.

If he only knew what he did to her. He had trained her body to want and to respond to him and him only.

He made his way up her back while laying pleasant kisses all over. He then turned her over onto her back. He straddled her as he stared at her beautiful face. He started placing more pleasant kisses from the tip of her forehead down to her toes. He made his way back up sliding his tongue into her mouth. He reached over to the side of the bed and pulled out four black silk scarves.

Her eyes widened. Telling her not to make a sound he placed his finger to her mouth. He proceeded to tie all four of her limbs to the bed posts. Spread out with her body glistening she looked so beautiful to him. He retrieved the platter of fruit placing a strawberry up to her mouth and telling her to take a tiny bite. He took that same strawberry and trailed it down to her nipples. He circled her right nipple with the fruit making a moan escape from her mouth. He looked up at her reminding her he didn't want to hear a sound. He then circled her left nipple with the same strawberry and clasped his juicy lips around her right. He took greedy steady pulls making her moan and bounce up and down off the mattress. He peeked up at her eyes as he lightly slapped her hip and reminded her he wanted silence.

She hated but loved the silent foreplay. She would swear by him making her accept everything he did to her in silence it intensified the sensation. She wanted to scream out loud, yet she enjoyed the ultimate feeling he gave her in silence like he demanded.

He closed his eyes and enjoyed the feel of her nipple in his mouth while trying not to moan his damn self. He concentrated on her right nipple pulling and sucking even more knowing in any second his heaven was due to explode. And exploded was exactly what she'd done. Her body bucked up and down on the bed with her eyes rolling in the back of her head. When he let go of her nipple he looked at her eyes and saw the thousand tears sliding down the sides of her face.

He loved that weak look on her, knowing she couldn't do anything about what he was doing to her. Her body belonged to him. He leaned over her kissing every single last tear away. On his way down her body he stopped to pay special attention to her left nipple. He didn't want it to feel left out. He finally made his way down to the main attraction of her body. He stared at his heaven loving the sight of her. He placed juicy kisses to her face then slid his tongue inside to get a feel of her pearl tongue.

She started bucking before he could even get a good grip on her clit. He grabbed her thighs tight looked up at her giving her a look to let her knew not to fuck with him. As soon as he got a tight grip on her clit she exploded once again. He was the one who broke the silent code this time. He closed his eyes moaning, enjoying the taste of her cum sliding down his throat. He felt her nudging him with her knee. Never letting go of her clit he looked up at her. In her eyes there was nothing but tears, love, and pain all rolled up in one emotion. She gave him a look to let him know, if she had to be quiet so did he. He nodded his head and went back to sucking her clit. She threw her hips into his face and once he started moving his tongue back and forth real fast across her clit he thought she was going to break free and fly off the bed. Her pussy came so hard she squeezed her eyes shut shedding tears the entire time he drank her juices. After getting the last drop he kissed his way up her body. Her pussy juices looked so good on his lips. She pleaded with her eyes for a taste. He held his face close to hers letting her have her fun. He couldn't blame her for being addicted to the taste of her own pussy juice because he sure in the fuck was.

After she cleaned his face dry he untied the scarves. He tapped her leg so she could move and he stretched out in the middle of the bed. When she straddled him he reached above his head and tied her hands to the post. He gave her his crooked grin knowing she thought she was going to control the ride. But this was his show and she was his. He slid her pussy onto his dick and closed his eyes as he savored the feeling. He had missed his heaven so much. Even though he had her six weeks ago before the birth of his son he still felt as if it was their first time. His heaven was so tight and was made just for his dick. He controlled her ride with his hands gripping her hips making her ride him in a slow even motion. With her arms tied above his head her breast sat right above his face. He took the opportunity to grab a hold of her right nipple knowing she would soon be cumming. When he started sucking and moving her up and down real slow he felt her pussy muscles clamp around his dick. She gripped her pussy around his dick pulling him deeper and deeper in her pussy. And as soon as he felt his heaven muscles pulsating on his dick his hot seed started shooting deep inside of her. Once she felt his seed she started grinding even harder and cumming all over his dick.

Now when they locked eyes she wasn't the only one with tears. He grabbed the back of her head and devoured her mouth. She started giggling while she kissed him.

"What the hell is so funny?"

"You thought you were going to be able to control that nut of yours. Thought you were going to pull three or four out of me with your dick before you came once." She kissed his soft lips, "Don, it's time for you to realize just like you control the heaven between my legs, I control the hell between yours. That baby will cum whenever my pussy demands him to."

He smiled at her, "You know what Doll, you're absolutely right. After what just happened I can't even argue with you on that one."

He untied his Queen and led them to the bathroom so they could take a shower with him cleaning the both of them.

TWENTY EIGHT

Sincere pulled up to his baby girl's father's mother's house. She had gotten in touch with Cherokee telling her she doesn't care about her son being a dead beat. She still wanted to be a part of her granddaughter's life.

Cherokee went inside to get her daughter only coming back outside empty handed. She came back to the car telling him Shereé refused to leave without him meeting her grandma Jackie.

As soon as he stepped through Jackie's front door and she turned to meet him she immediately threw her hands up to her mouth. Looking like she had seen a ghost she hollered and jumped up and down. "Oh my God, Oh my God"

Sincere and Cherokee looked at each other then back at Jackie like she was crazy.

She ran to Sincere and threw her arms around him, "Oh my God Sincere, I haven't seen you since you were like five years old. But I know it's you your face hasn't changed a bit."

Now he really had a strange shocked look in his face. This woman knew his name, remembered his face and hadn't seen him in seventeen years. He didn't know what to do so he just stood there and so did Cherokee.

Shereé ran to her grandmother and Sincere. "Grandma, how do you know my God-Daddy?'

Jackie looked at her second oldest grandchild responding, "Your God-Daddy, I don't know about all that but he is your cousin."

Cherokee finally spoke after hearing that. "Now what was that?"

"I said her cousin. Actually his mother Simone, God rests her soul, and I are first cousins."

Neither Sincere nor Cherokee could believe their ears. Cherokee thought *no wonder her daughter looked so much like him, they were related.*

All Sincere heard was that she was his mother's first cousin.

"You're my mother's cousin?"

"Yes Sincere, I'm also your cousin and my son who is Shereé dad is your cousin."

"I got that part. My baby girl turns out to be my flesh n blood which is why our bond is so strong. But what I want to know is if you are my mother's cousin, why haven't you seen me since I was five?"

"Well to make a long story short your mother and I both got lost in the mean streets thinking we were grown. Well my grown ass got addicted to crack so you can run with your imagination about what happened to me. Your mother on the other hand got addicted to a man, your father. She used to leave you with her friend Innocence all the time while she chased behind his punk ass."

His ears really perked up, "You're saying that like you know him."

"Know him, boy please. I grew up with him. I didn't grow up on Kinsman with Simone I was raised on Quincy. His daughter's mother and I were good friends until I got addicted to that shit."

Sincere grabbed his big cousin's hand, led her to the couch and sat down beside her, "Can you tell me about him?"

"Sure I can lil Sin. Where do you want me to start?"

"From the very beginning"

And that's exactly what Jackie did. She went all the way back from when his father's family migrated up to Cleveland from Alabama.

❊❊❊❊❊❊❊

Promise finally let Divine up for air because she was missing their son. As they drove to Innocence's house she thought it was time for her to come clean about the Rob and Black thing. She hated keeping lies from him, especially unnecessary ones at that. She gave him the short version of Rob turning out to be crazy.

He smiled at the fact that his Baby Doll was finally coming clean, "Doll, I already knew Rob had killed Black."

She looked over at him, "What the hell did you just say?"

"I said I already knew he was the one who killed Black. Did you forget I was doing my homework on the nigga you were having breakfast with? At first I thought

Rob killing him was just about business. But as I watched his mannerisms around you, I knew there was more to it. That's when I knew for sure besides the fact that you turned nine months I had to end his life, getting him away from you and my son."

She looked at him like he was the craziest man on the face of the earth. "What the hell you mean you watched him around me?"

He chuckled, "I mean exactly what the fuck I said. Oh you mean to tell me you honestly did think you were getting away with something when you were sneaking around with that nigga? Divine Nanette let me put you on to some game. Yes your nickel slick ass is the baddest bitch in the game but you never can out slick me. There's not a move you make that I don't know about. Just like with his brother Tone. I know you and Sincere took him out and I know you've been flooding Cedar with our dope through your little brother Jay."

She sat there with a shocked look on her face. How in the hell did he know about that. It had to be Sincere.

"Close your mouth and stop the wheels from turning in your head. Sincere didn't tell me shit. My cousin has a bond with you that I really don't understand. If I was really a crazy jealous nigga I would flip the fuck out on y'all but I can honestly say the loyalty y'all have with each other is totally innocent. Like him trying to keep me occupied while you went to that muthafucka's funeral. Trust me, I've been watching y'all. But like I say I know it's all innocent. Hell, he will do anything to keep you out of trouble not wanting me to put my foot in your ass. His loyalty to you would never allow him to tell me shit you do. And I didn't flip out about the Cedar thing y'all put together because I have been seeing the profits coming my way. That's when I figured y'all weren't doing no under handed shit. Your ass just didn't want to tell me you had a crazy nigga on your team."

He reached over and grabbed her hand, "And like I was saying I knew it was time to get his crazy ass away from you. Yeah he did serve a purpose. I let him keep you busy while I took care of other stuff. But then I started seeing things I knew you never would. Baby I can tell he had a whole fantasy world about you and him in his head. Now I will admit I'm crazy about you also, as Sincere would say retarded. And as you know I will kill every man on this planet about your ass. But what I won't do is ever hurt you. I would rather make you watch me kill, then that way you will know to stop playing with me. But that nigga Rob, once he would have figured out your heart didn't belong to him he would have rather seen you dead than with another man. That's that punk shit. If I can't have you then no one else can either. And you know I wasn't having that. So the nigga had to go."

He glanced her way again as he sat at the 140th light and he thought he saw fear in her eyes. "Baby, please don't tell me now you're scared of me?"

She leaned across the seat and placed a juicy kiss on his lips, "Never scared of you, just a little worried about what goes on in that head of yours sometimes."

"Crazy psychotic shit but as long as you know, I would never hurt you."

She gave him another peck, "I know you won't baby."

❊❊❊❊❊❊

Sincere was overwhelmed with the things his big cousin had told him. He honestly couldn't believe some of the things she said about his mother. Innocence never told him things like that. She knew he would have wanted to know everything about his mother, whether they were good or bad. Then he thought about how his mother seemed to live another life outside of her Kinsman life. What other reason could it have been for her best friend never being introduced to her son's father? And that son was alive and breathing for five years before she died. Yeah his mother definitely led a double life.

He couldn't wait to talk to his Twin and confide in her about the things he learned about his mother and his father.

❊❊❊❊❊❊

Divine walked inside of her Innocence's house ready to lie down on the couch with her son on her chest. Promise had drained all of her energy physically and mentally.

As soon as she lay down with her son she heard her ring tone letting her know she had a text message.

Promise picked up her phone and read the message and looked at her side ways. "Sincere want to know if you can meet him at his apartment. He says he really needs you, more than he ever has."

He stood over her handing her phone to her with that crazed look in his eyes. "Please don't tell me you're going to make me put down my own family, Baby Doll?"

She stared at the man she loved wholeheartedly. She loved everything about him. She loved his loving, caring, gentle heart, loyal side and she also loved his overprotective, aggressive, heartless, fearless side. She even loved his fucked up non remorseful psychotic side. But now this motherfucker had her fucked up. She lifted her son from her chest and gave him a juicy kiss on his forehead. She laid him down in his carrier and begun to gather his things.

Promise stared at her wondering what the fuck she was doing. He was about to snatch her up by her neck but then thought against it. They were at his mother's house. He would deal with his Queen in the privacy of their home. He laid down on the couch not giving a fuck about her tantrum because he meant what the fuck he had said.

After she got her son and her things together she left her Innocence's house and jumped into Promise's truck.

Once she was on the road she made a couple of phone calls.

Calling….Sincere
"Doll, a nigga need you for real, where you at?"
"I'm about to drop Knowledge off. Then I'm on my way to you."

"Alright"
Call ended....

Calling....Grandma
"Hello"
"Hey Grandma, I need a favor. Can you watch Boo Man for a little while for me?"
"Yeah Baby, bring him on."
"Thanks Grandma"
Call ended....

Calling....Da Don
"Yup"
"I don't know what the fuck is going on in your head. Not even an hour ago you said Sincere and I had an innocent bond that you didn't understand. Hell, I don't understand it either. But what I do understand and so should you if you even breathe too hard in his direction I would be the one putting yo ass down."
Call ended....

✦✦✦✦✦✦✦

After Divine left Sincere her mind was all over the place. But now she had to go inside her house and deal with Promise crazy ass. Her grandmother had already given her a call telling her he picked up Boo Man about an hour after she dropped him off.

Once she entered the house she went straight to Knowledge's nursery to give him a kiss but he wasn't there. She then went into her bedroom and saw Promise sitting up in the bed with his back against the headboard. He was holding Knowledge on his chest burping him. She walked over to them leaned down and gave her baby a gentle kiss on the forehead. She then cupped Promise's chin tilting his head back and giving him a fat juicy wet kiss on his lips. She rubbed her hand on his low trimmed beard as she slid her tongue into his mouth. She stood undressing while staring into his eyes and then walked toward the bathroom slowly so he could see all that belonged to him.

She sat in the tub with her knees pulled to her chest thinking.

Promise came into the bathroom kneeling down beside the tub. He reached in the water, grabbed her wash cloth, the pink dove soap and began to wash her.

She knew he was coming. She had been awaiting his arrival. That was his thing, washing her body. It was a habit he had formed from the first time he ate her pussy at their trap house. She loved for him to wash her. She had gotten so used to it that she hated when they were separated and she had to do it herself.

She stood so he could clean his heaven and her big juicy ass that kept his tongue hanging out of his mouth. He washed, rinsed, dried, and put lotion on her body while never speaking a word.

He led her to the bed helping her settle her naked body in. He left out of the room to check on his son making sure his baby monitor was on. As soon as he climbed into the bed with Divine he pulled her to him wrapping his arms around her neck, putting her face in his chest and throwing his leg over her body.

"Start talking!"

TWENTY NINE

Divine sat on the couch holding and admiring her son. It has become one of her everyday rituals. He was so beautiful. She thought about when she heard of mothers harming their children. How could someone hurt something so precious?

She then thought of her life and her relationship with her dad. *He was the first man she had ever loved. He was her Dad. She could remember him always being in her life and being there for her. Her mother Victory had told her a story of him not claiming her when she was pregnant with her. But she would never have thought that because he had always showed her much love.*

Her mother told her how on her first day home from the hospital she was surprised by an unexpected guest.

Fifteen year old Victory sat on the side of her bed admiring her newborn baby girl inside of her bassinet. She felt as if her daughter was the most perfect beautiful human being she had ever laid her eyes on. She promised right at that moment she would not become a statistic like a lot of teenage mothers she knew. She stroked her baby girl's cheek promising her she was going to finish school, get a good job, and would always provide for her. She told her daughter that she didn't have to worry about not having a father in her life because she was going to show her more love than two parents ever could. And she meant every word she spoke to her daughter.

She was pulled from her conversation with her baby by the sound of the bell. She made sure her baby was secure in her bassinet before going to answer the door. She was shocked when she opened the door and none other than Jason Dawson walked through.

He smiled at her asking if he could see the baby. She wasn't the type of woman to hold grudges so she decided she would let him.

She stood over her daughter's bassinet and told him there she was. She felt his arms from behind hugging around her waist. He began to tell her how beautiful his baby was and how she looked just like him.

Tears had begun to fall from her eyes. Her feelings were so hurt that he ever doubted her. He was the only guy she had ever slept with. When she first told him she was pregnant he was happy. But when she showed up at his apartment building with her outrageous belly in front of her she had gotten her heart broken into a thousand pieces. His mother was there and unbeknownst to her another female carrying his child. His mother pointed to the other female's stomach telling her that was his baby not hers. And ever since that day he didn't claim her child anymore. And then there he stood behind her claiming his daughter was beautiful looking just like him.

He left promising her he was going to be a good father and was going to always take care of his Lil Fat Momma.

She could honestly say he did. He came and got his daughter every weekend taking her to the other pregnant female's house that she had seen with his mother that day. The *other female turned out to be his woman who he shared an apartment with in the same building as his mother. And as his mother said that was his baby in her stomach. She gave birth to a daughter six months after Divine was born.*

When Divine turned five she not only stayed on the weekends but also spent entire summers with her dad. And that was around the time she could think back and have her own memories about her father.

She could remember her father always taking his Fat Ma everywhere he went. Even to all his women's houses. Where he was, she was. Where he laid his head on whatever night, she laid hers there also.

She had always been close to her dad. Hugging him, giving him kisses, even jumping in his lap when she hasn't seen him for days. It was nothing for her to fall asleep watching movies in the bed with him and her little brother Jay. He was her dad.

He taught her everything about the streets, men, and even herself. He discussed female hygiene with her piggy backing on what her mother had already taught her. When she turned thirteen he was the one that suggested to her mother that it was time for her to start seeing a gynecologist.

But all that perfect daddy's little spoiled, unconditional love, undeniable loyalty, dope man's little girl, relationship went crashing down.

On a Friday night she lay in her bed at her father's house unable to sleep.

As long as she had been spending weekends and summers with her dad she had never been alone at night in the house with him and then she never realized how close she and Jay had become. He was five years younger than her but they always had a good time together at their dad's house. But that particular night he wasn't there with her. Whom she felt was the reason why she couldn't sleep.

She couldn't fall asleep to save her life. But after watching movie after movie and counting stacks of money for her dad she finally fell into a deep sleep. In her sleep she felt a hand inside her panties. She thought she was dreaming until she felt his lips against her ear and heard his voice whispering, "Fat Ma if we do it, will you tell?"

Her eyes flew open and she jumped out of bed.

The television being on gave her room some light so when her eyes finally adjusted she saw her father sitting up in her bed. And for some odd reason she focused on the clock next to her bed reading 2:33am. She immediately started screaming and picking up things off her dresser and throwing them at him. He jumped out of her bed running out her room trying to block his head.

As she stood in the corner of her room not knowing what to do she heard the bathroom sink water running. She really couldn't comprehend what the hell had just happened to her.

She heard the water stop and she reached under her bed for the metal bat she kept there.

She saw her father easing into her room. She vaguely heard him begging and pleading. He told her how sorry he was, he was drunk, he didn't mean it, it would never happen again, and please don't tell anyone.

He left her room and returned with the duffel bag she placed in his room after she finished counting his money. He sat the bag on her floor begging her to take it and never to tell what happened. That time when he left her room he also left the house.

She was still standing in the corner finally grasping what the fuck had happened to her.

Her father had tried to steal from her He tried to take the most precious thing from her. She glanced at the duffel bag knowing what was inside.

She called her mother and asked her to pick her up telling her she was alone in the house and couldn't sleep.

Fat Momma left taking the duffle bag with her and keeping her Dad's dirty little secret.

But Divine Nanette left vowing that shit was far from over.

For some odd reason thinking about her past made her miss her father. Yes he hurt her but she didn't quite hate him. She could honestly say she wouldn't be who she was if it wasn't for all the life lessons he had taught her. And besides he was her Dad, she was his Lil Fat Momma and now he was a grandfather.

She picked up her phone deciding to give him a call. She went through her contact list because she didn't know his number by memory. Why would she, she never used it. But every time he changed numbers he gave the new number to her grandmother. And she kept it on hand telling herself just in case.

Her Dad had always tried to keep in contact with her. He was still putting money in the savings account he and her mother had started when she was young. Whenever the account got to a certain amount she would draw it down putting the money away for a rainy day. She had never told anyone what happened to her except for

Promise and when she did speak of her Dad it was never in an ill way. And that went vice versa for him also. Anyone talking to either one of them would think they still had the perfect father daughter relationship.

No one would have ever guessed they hadn't seen or talked to each other in the past seven years. Not even her mother and grandmother. She guessed it helped out a lot that he spent most of his time out of town.

When she found the name Father in her phone she pressed the call button.

JD felt his Blackberry vibrating on his waist. He looked at the number and didn't recognize it. But he always answered numbers he didn't know just in case one day his Fat Momma decided to call him.

THIRTY

Promise had an eerie feeling about the day. He didn't like the fact that Divine was going to see her father. But for some reason he didn't think that was why he was feeling off. There was something else brewing in the air. He thought it could be his birthday coming up. Being an April's fool baby was a notion in itself. Everyone tried playing tricks on him for the entire day ever since he could remember. Even his Baby Doll, but that wasn't it either. He said fuck it and continued on with his day.

He decided he would make a couple of money pick-ups then drop by his spot on 146th and fuck with his OG Pops.

Pops had always been around since Promise could remember. He had even helped mold Promise in the drug game. He really looked up to the old cat.

Pops has lived on 146th since forever but for the likes of him Promise couldn't remember ever being inside his house. He was old school and played by a different set of rules. And one of them was he didn't care how close he was with someone no one ever entered his home. He did dabble with dope himself but he was considered what some called a functional addict. He controlled his life not the dog food. But it was one thing Pops didn't play about and that one thing was Promise.

Promise pulled in front of his trap spot getting ready to dial Pop's number so he could come out of his house from across the street, but something caught his eye. He thought his eyes had to be deceiving him. He hadn't seen that broad since last August. After he had her suck his dick for the last time, really not doing shit for him he decided to cut them ties. All his time and energy went on getting his shit together for his Queen and his young God. He did try doubling back on her ass to straighten her out when Baby Doll told him she answered his phone but he found she had moved out. So he hadn't thought twice about the broad. But why in the fuck was she sitting outside his trap spot?

He jumped out of his car and walked to the passenger side of her car. She unlocked her doors so he could sit down. But he didn't open the door he just tapped on the window gesturing for her to follow him. He wanted to talk to her inside his spot not out in her car for all to see. He still had a bone to pick with her about his phone.

He walked into his spot and dismissed his brother Dre and a couple of soldiers telling them to leave the door cracked as he walked in the back to use the bathroom.

Dre yelled to the back with his face screwed up, "Big Homie why the hell you want the door cracked?"

He yelled over the sound of his piss hitting the water, "Because that broad Carmen is on her way up."

Dre shook his head at his brother as he walked out of the door. The nigga would kill anything moving about Baby Doll's ass, but yet he did shit to piss her off pushing her in the other direction.

When he passed Carmen on the stairs Dre looked at her knowing there was about to be some shit. So he decided he wasn't going too far.

She got comfortable on the couch waiting for him to come out of the back room. She could hear him rambling around back there.

When he finally emerged from the back all he could see was the back of her head over the couch.

"What's this I hear about you answering my muthafuckin' phone awhile back?"

She turned to look at him, "Hello to you too. And that was so long ago boy, I don't remember that." She then turned back around fumbling with something.

He wanted to shoot the bitch in the back of her head. He didn't care how long ago it was. Disrespecting in his heart was a fucking no, no.

When he walked around to the front of the couch his eyes widened, "What the fuck is that?"

"Why you got to be so ignorant all the time? This is your daughter," she responded while taking the cover off her daughter's face. She's four weeks today. I had her a couple weeks early. My doctor said she came a little early because I was stressing so much."

He didn't hear a word she had said. All he saw was his twin squirming around in her arms. He knew that looking at newborn babies the features could be a little iffy. But he knew that right there belonged to him. *Fuck, Baby Doll is going to kill my ass.*

"Okay I ain't the type of nigga that would deny my flesh and blood so you ain't got to worry about that. But why in the fuck would you keep this from me?"

"I knew if I told you I was pregnant you were going to try and make me have an abortion not wanting your so called Queen to find out and all."

"So if that's the case why the fuck are you here now? Because you do know my Queen still and will always come first?"

She smacked her lips rotating her neck, "You mean to tell me she comes before your daughter, Donnie?"

He stared at her thinking about the name she just called him. This bitch didn't know him from Adam or Eve, stupid Bitch.

He let two go once again, "POP" "POP". Nothing would ever come between him and Divine.

He dialed his brother's number.

"Yeah Big Homie, I saw that potential problem on my down the stairs. Now how the fuck are you going to explain that shit to Baby Doll?"

"I ain't got to explain shit. Now we got a clean-up in aisle two. Let's make this shit happen now."

❦❦❦❦❦❦

Jason had missed his Lil Fat Momma something crazy. He was truly sorry for what he did to her that night. He was drunk and he didn't know what he was doing but at the same time he kind of did. But if it was any consolation he was truly and very sorry he hurt his daughter.

He was so fucking happy when he heard her voice on the other end of his phone telling him she missed him and wanted to see him. And when she told him he was a grandfather he was really overjoyed. At the time when she called he was actually out of town but he told her he was coming back to Cleveland ASAP to see his baby and grandchild.

He waited for her to arrive at his house in Chagrin Falls that no one knew about. It was his secret hide out when he didn't want to be bothered. He was juggling so many women, had so many kids, and was still doing his one, two in the streets. He needed a place to get away to sometimes.

He heard her pull in the driveway. He jumped off the couch pulling the door open ready to reunite with his daughter.

As soon as she reached the door Divine jumped into her father's arms just like she did when she was younger. He wrapped his arms around her pulling her into the house and swinging her around in a circle.

She cried on her father's shoulders as he held her, "Dad, I've missed you so much. My life hasn't been right since we haven't been seeing each other. I know you didn't mean to hurt me. Dad, I know you didn't."

He put her down and looked into her teary eyes.

Shedding tears his self, "Fat Ma I love you and I'm so sorry. Daddy never meant to hurt you."

She stood there staring as if she was looking straight through him. Hearing that name come out of his mouth took her to another place, and Daddy, he damn sure wasn't her Daddy. That title belonged all to Promise. All day every day, hell she had never in her life ever called him Daddy. Every since she could comprehend she knew calling him daddy wasn't right. That was what all those young girls called him when they stopped on or rode down Central. So he was always her Dad, never her Daddy.

"Do you hear me Fat Ma? I promise it will never happen again."

She blinked out of her trance, "Yeah Dad I'm sorry. I heard you. But we don't ever have to travel down that road again okay. Let's leave the past in the past."

"You're right Fat Momma, but where is my grandbaby. I thought you were bringing him with you."

"I did. He's in the car with his Dad. I wanted to get our emotional part out before I brought them in. So are we cool now? We're done with the tears, right?"

"Yes we are. Now call that man and tell him to bring me my grandson."

She did as her father asked.

He walked through the door carrying the baby's car seat. He sat the car seat down and held out his hand introducing himself to Baby Doll's father.

"How you doing sir, it's nice to finally meet you. Divine has told me so much about you."

Jason just stood there staring. The young man looked so familiar to him, he just couldn't place him. He was praying he wasn't who he thought he was. That would be a disaster for his daughter to somehow have hooked up with him.

Divine waved her hand in front of her dad's face, "Um Dad, hello! What's wrong do you do know him or something?"

"Nawl, Fat Ma. He just looks so much like a guy I used to know." Jason responded as he shook his grandson's father's hand.

She stood beside her father looking at him with disgust in her eyes, "Don't you mean he looks so much like a girl you used to know?"

Jason let go of his hand chuckling nervously praying once again that the guy wasn't who he thought he was. "No Fat Ma, I mean guy. Now let me get a look at my grandbaby." He bent down removing the blanket from the car seat.

He looked on in shock. He looked up to Divine and saw an emotion he hadn't seen on her face in seven years. "Um, um, Fat Ma you want to tell me what's going on. There ain't no um, um, baby in there."

"What the fuck you think is going on? Now sit yo stuttering ass down and shut the fuck up."

Who the fuck did she think she was. He knew he fucked up, but he was still her damn father. "Who the fuck do you think you talking to? I'm your God-damn daddy."

She gave him her evil grin. She was glad he was putting up resistance because she wouldn't have had it any other way. This was big bad JD right here. She would have felt a certain way if he would have bitched up following orders.

She pulled out her nine and slapped him across the face with the handle. "You ain't my damn daddy so stop saying that shit. I ain't one of your tricking hoes you used to have out on that stroll."

Jason held his face in pain. He couldn't believe she did that shit. And he wasn't going to believe what she was about to do next.

She gave him another grin then shot him once in each leg.

He buckled down to the floor screaming like a bitch. "Fuck you Divine! I've already suffered and apologized enough for what I did to you, but it doesn't matter no more. Now just go ahead and kill me because if you don't I'm telling you I'm going to kill your disrespectful ass."

"As much as I would love to kill you, I'm not. I'm going to leave that to my big brother." She turned grabbed the car seat and headed out of the door, "Handle yo business."

Jason smiled at his oldest son, "When you first walked through that door I had a feeling that was you. You look a lot like your mother but I see myself all in you. So since I know you are your father's son go ahead and pull that trigger just like I did to yo trickin' ass momma. You and your sister playing these punk ass games, I'm motherfucking Jason Dawson, you think I give a fuck about you. You ain't shit but a whore's son…" "POP", another shot in the leg.

"Fuck….nigga say what you got to say and handle yo business. Ain't no point in prolonging this shit."

"You right, but before I do I want you to know this isn't for my mother. I've learned to live with her absence and I was finally told y'all history. I ain't green to the game. Her young ass got addicted to that shit and started cheating you out yo money because you weren't claiming or taking care of your son. So if it means anything to you I want you to know I'm killing yo punk ass for my Doll. You had to be one sick fucker to try and fuck your own daughter. Any nigga doing shit like that doesn't deserve to live."

"POP"! One last shot straight to the head.

He looked down at the man who was supposed to be his father.

He spat on him and walked over his body. He looked back at him feeling no remorse for the man. He walked out of the front door signaling the clean-up team to come and do their job not giving a fuck about a JD.

He sat in the car looking over at Divine. He reached across putting his arm around her neck pulling her to him. "Damn, all these years we've been cool, kicking it together, getting money together, me protecting you, you protecting me, and I'll be damn if we ain't brother and sister. Now ain't that some shit."

She kissed Sincere on the cheek, "Yup, ain't that some shit. I guess that's where our bond came from that no one could understand."

"I guess so Twin. I guess muthafuckin so."

EPILOGUE

For the past two years Divine had turned herself into a homebody leaving the streets for Promise. But for the past week her life had been havoc. She had been ripping and running like something crazy. She took their clothes to the cleaners, did the grocery shopping, the laundry, cleaned and dusted the entire house from top to bottom. And she even played school. On top of all that she and Promise hadn't spent much quality time together nevertheless had sex.

She wasn't trying to complain about her new role she was playing because that's what she wanted. To be home with her family and start herself a business, but she was in desperate need of some R and R. Not to mention she had been missing her new best friend so she figured she'd let Innocence play school for the day and plan her and Cherokee a day at the spa.

"What's up Kee, what you doing?"

"Nothing bored as hell. Why, y'all about to come over?"

"Just me, and I'm already outside. Slide on some clothes and let's ride."

"Give me 'bout 20 and I'll be out there."

"K"

Promise was so tired of the streets he didn't know what to do. All week he have been doing drop-offs and pick-ups and he was mad as shit because the money from Cedar was coming up short. Ten thousand short to be exact which was very unacceptable in his book. He'd been trying to work with Jay about the money but the little nigga thought because he's Divine's little brother he didn't have to answer to anybody. But soon he was going to get a rude awakening fucking around with Promise. He doesn't give a damn about him being her blood and if Jay doesn't straighten up his act soon he was going to see Promise's ugly side.

Promise walked into the house with the weight of the world on his shoulders but once he entered his bedroom and saw his Queen lying across the bed with her legs spread open dipping her fingers in and out of his heaven it seemed as though all his stress went away.

He walked over to the edge of the bed so he could get a closer look.

"Daddy, aren't you going to join me?"

"I think I'm going to stand here and enjoy the view."

Divine spread her pussy lips wider so he could get that view he had just mentioned. "Please Daddy you know she doesn't respond to me. Heaven wants you and you only. She misses you terribly. You haven't touched her in a week, not that I'm complaining I know you've been busy taken care of business but I also know she would help relax you." She dipped her finger inside her pussy brought it out and circled her fat clit. "Please Daddy."

He dropped to his knees not being able to resist the site before him and the way she was begging he couldn't deny his Queen. He looked up at her from between her big healthy thighs. "Mommy I love you so fucking much and you should know by now that you don't have to beg. I'll give you any and every thing you want." With that being said he lowered his head to get him a taste of his heaven.

He ate her pussy like he was in a contest. He licked her clit up, down, and in circles and the moment she felt his lips tighten around her clit sucking her life away she arched her back, grabbed his head, and screamed his name.

He drunk every ounce of her sweet juice begging with his tongue for her to give him more and that's exactly what she did, cumming in his mouth two more times.

He looked up at his Queen loving the look of fulfillment on her face, "Do you want a taste?"

She gave him a devilish smile, "Yes Daddy and I want more than a taste."

By the time he finished fucking and cleaning his Baby Doll he didn't want to nothing but sleep the entire night through.

He heard his phone vibrating on the night stand. He reached for his phone checking out the time on the alarm clock. "Damn its 7 o'clock in the morning." He answered his phone, "This better be good."

"P, you need to get up we got a situation."

He listened to all the details Sincere gave him. "You handle it 'til I get there. I have to get my family together. I'm bringing Baby Doll in on this one too because something got to shake, that shit just don't sound to right."

"That's exactly what I'm saying", Sincere responded as he hung up the phone.

Divine was awakened with little hands playing with her cheeks and with her eyes still shut tight she smiled knowing exactly who they belonged to. As she slowly opened her eyes she saw the most beautiful set of eyes staring at her.

"Good morning"

Her baby giggled at her. Divine snuggled her baby close to her so that they were face to face. As she looked upon her child she admired everything about her baby's perfect little face. The skin complexion, the hazel brown eyes, the little juicy kissable cotton soft lips, and the long naturally curly hair that she knew she was going to have hell trying to tame in years to come.

She kissed her baby's small forehead, "I love you Treasure Marie."

When Promise had brought the baby girl to her at only four weeks old she never asked him any questions. Anyone who has ever laid eyes on her knew she belonged to Promise. Treasure looked so much like her father that she even shared the soul stealing stare that he had. The reason she never questioned the mother's whereabouts was because she knew her man and she knew him well. Just as he wouldn't let another man walk the earth claiming to be Knowledge's real father he wouldn't let another woman walk the earth claiming to have had a baby with him.

His Treasure belonged to his beloved Divine. He even went so far as to find out which hospital she was born in, the exact date and the exact time. Then picking up a copy of her birth certificate from City Hall, he had his lawyer to draw up some legal papers stating that the mother Carmen Gray had given up all her parental rights to her child never wanting to have anything to do with her. He then changed his baby girl's name from Donetta Gray to Treasure Marie Green. Once all of that was in order he had his lawyer draw up more papers for Divine to legally adopt his daughter. They didn't have to go through all those changes with their son because Divine was the mother giving birth and Promise was the man there signing the birth papers making Knowledge his. Promise's name was the actual name that appeared on his son's birth certificate.

She smiled at their baby girl giving her another kiss on her forehead. "Baby Girl, where is your Dad and brother?"

Her daughter giggled at her once again. Even though Treasure was twenty five months old and Knowledge was twenty eight months old she always talked to them with full complete sentences. She never used baby talk with her children.

"Okay Baby Girl, where is Boo man?"

Hearing her brother's name made Treasure smile from ear to ear she sat up and pointed towards the door, "down."

"He's downstairs with your daddy? Well that's where we might need to be then."

Divine got out of bed and went into the bathroom to take care of their breath.

Once they made it half way down the stairs she smelled the aroma of breakfast being prepared.

Promise smiled at his Queen as she came into the kitchen with their daughter on her hip. He loved the relationship the two of them shared. One would never guess that another female's blood ran through his daughter's veins. His Baby Doll treated his Baby Girl as if she had birthed her herself.

He walked to them taking his daughter from Divine's arms and giving her a kiss on the forehead and giving Divine a juicy kiss on the lips.

She gave her son a kiss as they sat down at their family breakfast nook ready to begin with their breakfast.

Promise blessed the food then giving his attention to Divine. "After we're finished with breakfast we need to drop the kids off to Innocence."

Taking a bite of her turkey bacon she asked, "Why are we doing that? It's Sunday, their day to spend time with both of us. No business on Sundays. Family time remember? That's your rule."

"I know Mommy, but Sincere called when you were sleep. He said that Jay spot was raided around six this morning, but no one was arrested. They just took all the money and all the dog food from the spot."

Divine wanted to scream but she knew she couldn't. Her babies were at the table with them. She smiled at her children as they enjoyed their cinnamon toast waffles. She looked at Promise asking through clenched teeth, "Why didn't you wake me up right after you talked to him? We could have had breakfast on the go."

He laughed at his Queen knowing she was ready to go into Boss Bitch mode, "Because I didn't. My children are going to at least enjoy breakfast with us this morning at home seeing as though we're going to be busy for the rest of the day. And Sincere is already there handling things."

He stood to clear his space at the table. He stared at Divine with don't fuck with me eyes, "Don't ever question me again about why I didn't do shit. Now when my seeds are finished eating I'll get them ready to go over their grandmother's house while you get the kitchen together, then I will take care of you."

He started walking away but stopped to look back at Divine needing to make sure she understood what the fuck he had said to her. "Don't ever question me again Baby Doll. My family will always come first. I don't give a fuck about what's going on. Do you understand me?"

She smiled knowing he was absolutely right. Their family did come before any of their recreational shit.

"Yes Daddy, "she responded gazing at her King thinking *how much she loved* **HER PROMISE**.

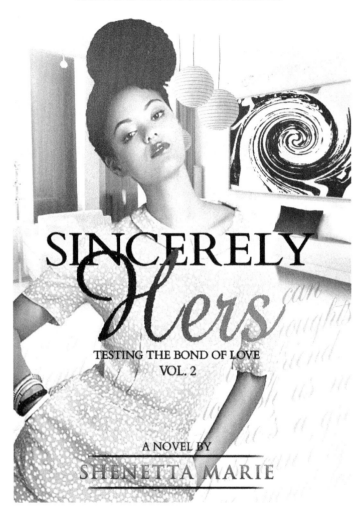

A DIVINE PRODUCTION PRESENTS

SINCERELY
Hers

TESTING THE BOND OF LOVE
VOL. 2

A NOVEL BY

SHENETTA MARIE

Available Now

A DIVINE PRODUCTION PRESENTS

LEGEND
BOSSES OF THE LAND

SHENETTA MARIE

Available Now

A DIVINE PRODUCTION PRESENTS

DOMINICAN CARTEL

THE SEQUEL TO LEGEND

SHENETTA MARIE

In The Lab

About the Author

Shenetta Marie born and raised in Cleveland, Ohio, is a mother of two wonderful sons. She loves to spend time with her family and close friends and is now embracing her new love, writing.

Feel free to visit the rising Author/Publisher @ www.adivineproduction.net
shenettamarie@yahoo.com
Follow her on twitter @shenettamarie
facebook Author Shenetta Marie
IG @shenettamarie

Made in the USA
Middletown, DE
24 March 2023

27053694R00136